The DEAD *Can* TALK

In the President's Service Series: EPISODE 6

Ace Collins

Ace Collins

Elk Lake Publishing
In the President's Service, Episode Six: The Dead Can Talk
Copyright © 2014 by Ace Collins
Requests for information should be addressed to:
Elk Lake Publishing,
Atlanta, GA 30024
ISBN-13 NUMBER: 978-1942513322

Cover and graphics design: Stephanie Chontos and Anna O'Brien
Editing: Kathi Macias
Cover Model: Alison Johnson
Photography: Ace Collins

CHAPTER I

Friday April 17, 1942
2:05 AM
Five miles north of Brighton, England

Shelton Clark was thirty-five, lean, and focused, and from his position in the front of the small boat, Clark's hazel eyes carefully scanned the British beach. It appeared deserted, but as the American agent had learned during his five months undercover in Germany, looks are often very deceiving. In times of war, eyes were everywhere, and they were almost always open. Ten days earlier he was sure he'd been spotted as he raced away from the chemical lab twenty miles outside of Berlin, and he was just as positive that in spite of the fire he'd help set to cover his tracks, the Nazis knew he had the formula, and that formula was worth more than his life. In fact it was worth more than the lives of millions. And that's why, armed only with a knife, he'd fought a member of the S.S. to the death to keep it. Therefore, even as an underground leader ferried him from France across the English Channel, he constantly looked over his shoulder. Perhaps he'd evaded the hoards that must have been tailing him. Perhaps the circuitous route taken across Germany and France had provided him with the cover he needed. But until he arrived at intelligence headquarters in London and met with OSS agent Russell Strickland, he could not be sure of anything other than there was a price on his head, and men with a price on their heads could never fully relax.

Pushing his right hand through his thick red hair, Clark glanced back at the man rowing the small boat across the choppy waters. Hans Holsclaw had to be over fifty, yet this short, unassuming, bald-headed man had the strength and stamina of a person half his age. Born in Holland, the blue-eyed rebel was a quiet, almost stoic soul who, far beneath his placid exterior, possessed keen instincts. He could literally smell danger and therefore always seemed to find a way to avoid direct contact with the enemy. But when he chose to strike, the results were so lethal the S.S. had pegged him "The Snake."

Since 1939, when his hatred for Hitler reached the boiling point, the Dutchman had blown up everything from bridges to factories and had set off firestorms from Italy to the North Sea coast. During that time more than a dozen Nazi officers simply disappeared, thanks to The Snake's bite, and scores of others were injured badly enough they would never return to the war. By 1942 the now seemingly mystical underground leader was blamed for every act of terror in Germany. And when Hitler spoke of the The Snake, he did so with such rage even the Fuhrer's loyal German shepherd raced from the room. Therefore it was no surprise that in meeting after meeting, Hitler demanded his generals apprehend and execute The Snake. But it was hard to catch a man whose identity was the best-kept secret in Europe, enabling the Nazi's most feared enemy to hide in plain sight.

On most days Holsclaw worked as a cobbler in Groningen, Holland. The German soldiers who passed his shop considered him nothing more than a businessman trying to hold onto his livelihood during times of war. He charmed the Nazis with his smile and gladly resoled their boots. They had no idea that on a recent day, when the business was closed, the diminutive shoe repairman was the force behind the explosion and fire that leveled Dr. Wilhelm Krantz's laboratory, destroying all the scientist's research on alternative fuel sources. In fact The Snake's bite was the last thing Krantz would experience on this earth.

"You are fearless," Clark said admiringly as the pair grew tantalizingly close to the English shore.

"I'm nothing more than a man fighting for my country," Holsclaw argued. "You are doing the same thing."

The American shook his head; in the past two weeks the cobbler had proven himself to be far more than just another man. Clark had grown to so admire the Dutchman's brains and grit that if the American were ever asked to go to hell and kidnap the devil, he'd make Holsclaw his team leader.

"It has been the greatest honor of my life to serve with you," Clark announced with a smile.

As he continued to row the small boat, the gentle waves lapping at the wooden hull, Holsclaw replied, "As my father, who was a Lutheran minister, always told me, it is an honor just to serve. I hope we will meet again at Hitler's graveside to celebrate a victory."

"I'll do my best to be there," the American assured him. "Now, my friend, you are almost home."

"No," Clark corrected him. "Home is a small town in Arkansas. What I am is almost back to safety. And it doesn't seem fair that I shall be safe and you will once more be working behind the lines."

Holsclaw shrugged. "We both have our places, and we both have our jobs. The information you are taking back will no doubt change the course of the war in our favor. So I believe your job is much more important than mine."

The sound of aircraft flying somewhere in the distance caused both men to shift their gaze to the cloudy skies. Though they couldn't see the planes, they knew where they were from as well as where they were going.

"London will feel Hitler's wrath again tonight," Holsclaw noted.

"The English are as tough as that leather you have in your shop," Clark assured him. "They'll withstand the attack and deliver a few blows of their own."

Shifting his eyes back to the beach, which was now only a hundred yards away, the American once more studied his landing point. Reaching into the pocket of his black leather coat, Clark felt for his pistol. Wrapping his right hand around the gun, he prayed he wouldn't have to use it. War had forced the quiet man to take too many lives. On this night he longed for peace.

"Just get me close enough to wade in," Clark suggested. "Then you need to get back to France and hurry to your business in Holland before the Nazis figure out who you really are. We need you far worse than we need me."

"The Allies need that formula more than either one of us," Holsclaw suggested.

There was no argument there. If Germany put Krantz's research to use, it could change the war's whole dynamic. With a war machine that had an endless supply of stable hydrogen power, the Allies would lose one of their greatest advantages — control of most of the world's energy resources. Thus the enemy would no longer need oil as their fuel source and could focus their efforts completely on weapon development and conquest.

Clark felt the boat scrape bottom, and as it did he looked back to his comrade and smiled. Tossing a quick salute, he reached out and shook the underground leader's hand.

"You are a good friend," Clark said.

"As are you," Hoslclaw replied. "Good luck." "God bless you."

As he released his grip, the American grinned, leapt over the edge and into the knee-deep water. Ignoring the cold sea soaking through his shoes, he quickly moved forward toward the beach. As he did, Holsclaw turned the boat and headed in the opposite direction.

A slight mist greeted the American as he slogged upon the slick, grass-covered shoreline. Reaching into his left pocket, he retrieved a small flashlight and turned it on and off three times. His visual message was answered with a trio of flashes from a hill. That meant Strickland was there to meet him.

7

Smiling, Clark slipped the light back into this jacket, released his grip on his gun, and moved toward the hill. He'd taken only three steps when a shot rang out, tearing into his right shoulder and knocking him to the ground. From seemingly out of nowhere, two large men, dressed in dark clothing, were upon him. As one held him down, the other hurriedly searched through his pockets.

"Nothing," a deep voice grumbled.

"Cut him open."

Pulling a large knife from his belt, the man pushed it forward, slicing not just Clark's coat and shirt, but also slashing into his stomach. The pain raced through his body with the power and speed of a locomotive rolling down a mountain grade. One, two, three times the man dug the blade into his gut. Tossing the large knife to one side, the assailant grabbed a flashlight from his coat. Just as he flipped it on, a series of shots rang out. The second one struck the man with the flashlight, knocking him sideways onto the sand.

Seemingly undeterred the other attacker pushed his hand into Clark's gut. A few seconds later, as even more bursts of fire rang out, the attacker cursed, leapt to his feet, and raced off into the night. And for a few seconds, the American was once more alone.

Though he no longer felt pain, Clark realized the almost soothing warmth he felt in his shoulder and stomach was blood rushing from his body and draining what little life he had left onto the English beach. He also knew he would not be meeting with Holsclaw to celebrate the end of the war, never again fish in the Ouachita River, never go to another movie, and never again kiss Connie Simmons. Most importantly he'd never again serve his country. Soon his life would always be remembered in the past tense.

As he patiently waited for death, Clark heard footsteps. A few seconds later Russell Strickland, a tall middle-aged man with closely cropped blond hair, jogged up to the wounded agent. Kneeling beside the person who was not just his partner in the O.S.S. but also his friend, Strickland announced, "You're okay. I'll get you to a doc who'll patch you up."

Clark forced a smile. At least he wouldn't be dying alone.

Somewhere in the distance Clark heard anti-aircraft fire and felt the concussions caused by bombs. The war would continue without him. Taking a final deep breath, he lifted his left arm and whispered, "Don't forget to check my pulse." After a wave of his right hand, he added, "Goodnight, sweet prince."

CHAPTER 2

Sunday April 25, 1942

1:15 AM

A small private airport ten miles outside Washington D.C.

"I had her in my sites," Alistar Fister complained as he plopped down on a wooden chair inside a metal barn that served as the airstrip's hanger. "Why didn't you let me kill her?"

Bauer leaned his tall lanky frame against the wall, crossed his arms, studied his companion for a few moments, shook his head, and spat onto the dirt floor. In spite of his body's ability to handle the drug, Alistar was becoming more trouble than he was worth. He was too impulsive and had no respect for authority. When Bauer found another suitable test subject, he'd gladly punch Alistar's extermination ticket.

"Alistar," Bauer quietly announced, "you need to get this through your thick skull. I own you. I decide when and where you do what you do. Your mission was to take out Lupino, not Helen Meeker. The next time you dare to change the orders, you'll pay with your life. Let me make this clear: there is no one in my world that is not expendable except me."

Alistar shook his head. "Meeker's much more the thorn in your side than Grace. Lupino is just a nuisance. She's like a pest that aggravates you rather than kills you." He paused as if trying to control his rage. "Besides, Meeker's supposed to be dead. I was just trying to make a lie the truth."

Bauer grinned. Alistar had finally hit on something. Meeker and her friends were ghosts and, in this modern age, who believes in ghosts? It was brilliant! In the middle of the war there was a transparent group of men and women working in the dark on special assignments likely given by the White House. This concept was better even than the radio hero *The Shadow*.

Bauer glanced out toward the vacant runway. "*Supposedly* dead is right. It appears no one that went down in that plane crash is really dead. In fact I doubt if there even was a plane crash." He rubbed his chin. "It seems the president is taking a page from my playbook. He figures the grave is the best hiding place for those who do his most important jobs."

"What good does it do them to supposedly be dead?" Alistar growled. "We know they're not."

A still grinning Bauer slowly turned to face his employee. "They don't know who knows. Yes, Meeker saw me; I wanted her to. But she didn't see you, so she won't be worried about you knowing she and the rest are alive." The tall man quickly closed the distance between himself and Alistar before adding, "For reasons I don't fully understand, I'm guessing Roosevelt felt a need to form a special operative group. You're killing Meeker would not have given me any insight as to what their mission is. So we have to watch and wait. I have a feeling if we study the other names from the crash, we'll find out who else is on their team."

"Why do you think FDR is behind this?" Alistar demanded.

"Because Meeker was his pet. She was the one woman who had his ear. He trusted her and is fully aware of her abilities and talents. The man you saw at the airport in Texas is likely part of the group as well."

"You mean Clay Barnes? He was one of the top men in the Secret Service."

"That ties in. I'm trying to remember who else died in that supposed plane crash." Bauer snapped his fingers. "The FBI agent we kidnapped!"

"Henry Reese?"

Bauer nodded. "He and Meeker were partners going back several years when she was attached to the FBI on a kidnapping case." Bauer paused and considered the three people he had identified. Each was unique and had a specialty, but there had to be more than just this trio. "Alistar, finding out who's on this team is vital. While Meeker, as you noted, is a bit of a thorn in our sides, this group could be much more. In fact they might exist just to bring my organization down. I have to know who they are and where they're based."

"And how do you propose to do that?"

"Right now they're interested in Lupino. They likely want her because they spotted her with you. Therefore whoever grabbed Grace tonight is going to take all their attention for a while. I got his car's license number and the make of the car, and with a properly placed phone call or two, we can get his identity."

"They can get the same information just as quickly," Alistar argued.

"Sure," Bauer admitted. "In truth they likely already know who he is. But I'd bet they're like us and don't know where he's taken Lupino. So we just need to get there before them. I've got men in D.C., and with one call they'll be working on it."

"But Lupino doesn't have the documents."

"Which means that whoever has Grace will soon discover they don't have anything of value. And she's not worth anything by herself."

Alistar threw his hands up in the air and growled, "But those documents were a ticket to big bucks for you."

The noise of a plane's motor caused Bauer to turn his gaze back out the hanger door. He listened for a few seconds before noting, "Our ride should be here in a couple of minutes." He looked back at his companion. "Those pieces of paper, the ones Meeker now has, are of little consequence to me. I don't care about them anymore than I do Lupino."

"I don't get you," Alistar rose from his chair and stomped out into the cool night air as he spoke. "You were giving those documents to Hitler. When that fell through you sent me to kill Grace, and now you say both of them mean nothing."

"If," Bauer suggested, "the U.S. government gets Grace and she talks, there's nothing she can tie to me. She doesn't even know what I look like. And when she's through singing, she'll either be executed or spend the rest of her days in a federal prison.

For all practical purposes her life is over. But I am interested in who wants her and why. That means I need the identity of the man behind the action tonight and the names of the people on Meeker's team."

Alistar watched as a single-engine Cessna dropped gracefully from the sky and set down on the flat grass-covered piece of pasture. As he studied the plane taxiing up to the hanger, Bauer laid a hand on his shoulder.

"You see," Bauer explained, "for the moment Meeker and I have the same objective. We both want to know who the third party is and what they think Lupino brings to the game."

The tall man picked up a small suitcase and ambled toward the plane. He'd only told Alistar the part of the story that actually made sense. The other part about reclaiming a lost love, even Bauer didn't fully understand that. But after seeing Meeker face-to-face, he was sure the words that only he had heard were true. And if that meant he was crazy, then he'd face that fact down the road.

CHAPTER 3

Monday April 27, 1942
10:55 PM
Magnolia, Arkansas

Dave Bost drove his 1939 Buick to Sherriff Ralph Watts' home and blew his horn. A few seconds later the short, wide lawman, still wearing his tan uniform and hat, stepped out onto the porch of the two-bedroom, white-frame home, strolled down three well-worn wooden steps, and hustled to the passenger door. After sliding into the front seat, Watts closed the door and looked over at his friend of more than twenty years.

"I can't believe you of all people would call me in the middle of the night to go to the cemetery. I mean, it's not like you're scared of ghosts. Or are you?"

Bost was used to being teased. Everyone seemed to enjoy picking on funeral directors. And as graveyards were his second home, he really had no fear of them. In many ways he found them comforting. But tonight he needed Watts, not to ward off specters, but to shed some illumination on a new grave.

"You got your flashlight?" Bost asked, his dark eyes shining in the glow of the instrument panel. Before his passenger could answer, the driver pulled out onto the street and headed south.

"It's on my belt," the lawmen assured him. "The batteries are fresh. But why do you need my light at Pleasant Hill? You know that place like the back of your hand."

The slightly built gray-headed undertaker didn't reply as he drove out of the city limits, took a right turn just past a sawmill, and steered the car onto a well-worn dirt road. Slowing to twenty in order to dodge puddles created by an afternoon thunderstorm, he turned on the radio. Thirty seconds later after the tubes warmed up, the news came on.

Eyewitnesses report that as many as fifty people died and hundreds more were injured when a huge tornado destroyed Pryor, Oklahoma, today. The massive storm struck with no warning and roared right through the community's main business district, felling buildings and hurling cars and trucks through the air as if they were children's toys.

Not asking permission the sheriff reached over to turn down the volume before soberly announcing, "I've seen storms like that. They show no mercy. About the only good thing they do is bring folks like you business. Guess we're lucky we've never had one like that here, except for the fact you might profit by it."

His eyes closing to slits to reveal a web of wrinkles in his cheeks and on his brow, Bost replied, "I know we've been friends for a long time, but that's not funny. I never wish for anyone's death."

"I think I know you well enough to know that. But let's face it. Your job and mine depend upon misfortune. You need folks to die, and I need someone to commit a crime, or else our services aren't required. We both may pretend it's not so, but we actually thrive off others' misery. It's just a fact."

Bost shrugged. Watts was right. The only time business came calling was during sad moments, and that wasn't something to brag about. But deep down he knew what both men did was also a service.

As the undertaker eased around a puddle large enough for a full-grown hog to wallow in, the lawman posed the question of the moment. "Now why do you need me to go to the cemetery with you?"

"Lost my wallet, Ralph," Bost explained. "And you have the best flashlight in
town."

"And you couldn't wait until tomorrow morning? After all, the sunshine is a lot brighter than my light."

"I put five-hundred dollars in that wallet this morning. That's not chickenfeed. I couldn't sleep with the thought of it sitting out in the open."

"Dave, are you sure you didn't leave it at the office or at home?"

"I've looked everywhere, even inside our display coffins and the trashcans, but it's not there. The last time I remember having it was at the memorial for Shelton Clark today. I'm guessing I must have dropped it after the workers filled in the grave."

"I hope you didn't drop it in the grave before they filled it up. I'm not digging anything or anyone up tonight."

"No," Bost assured him, "I pulled it out when Jim and Amos completed their work. So I had it when I paid them. I must have lost it when I straightened a couple of the floral displays. With your bright flashlight we'll likely find it in no time."

As Bost made a left into the century-old graveyard, the car's headlights splashed the old grounds with illumination. A second later Watts grabbed the driver's arm and whispered, "Stop the car."

As Bost pulled the sedan to a complete standstill, he glanced toward his companion. "Why?"

His body tense and his face showing sudden apprehension, the sheriff ordered, "Back out onto the road and head the way we came."

"But . . ."

"Don't ask questions; just do it."

Shaking his head, Watts jammed the shifter into reverse, backed onto the dirt road and, after placing the Buick into first, eased off on the clutch and headed east. Once they'd topped a hill and driven about halfway down, the lawman quietly announced, "Okay, pull over to the side. Kill the motor and lights, and let's walk back to the graveyard."

"In all my fifty-three years of living," Bost complained, "this is about the screwiest thing I've ever done. We aren't teenagers going to a graveyard to tip over the stones; we don't have to sneak in. I just need to find my wallet."

"Dave, as you pulled into the cemetery, your lights flashed onto a truck. Someone's in the cemetery, and I figured if it looked like we were just turning around, they wouldn't get spooked."

"Is that your attempt at a bad pun?"

"No. I'm not feeling funny right now. Now let's quietly get out of the car and sneak back down there. Whoever's there this time of the night can't be up to any good."

Suddenly a simple exercise in seek-and-find had grown a bit more ominous. Bost sensed the seriousness of the situation, not just by his friend's gloomy tone but also because Watts had now drawn his gun from the holster. Gently opening the door, the funeral director followed his stocky friend back up the hill. Stopping before the cemetery's entrance, the sheriff cut off through a muddy ditch, with Bost following him step by step. Standing behind an oak tree, Bost studied Watts as the sheriff observed the rear of a blue or black GMC pick-up truck sitting about fifty yards ahead. When the funeral director turned his attention to the truck, he noted something that alarmed even him.

"Dave," Bost whispered, "those guys just dug up Shelton Clark's coffin."

"Yep," the sheriff replied, "and it looks like they've loaded it into the truck. Now why would anyone want to steal Shelton's body?"

"I have no idea."

"As bodies are in your line of work," Watts continued, "I was hoping you'd give me a better answer than that."

"This isn't the time for jokes."

"Well, we can at least agree on that. You stay here. They're likely armed, and I don't want you risking your life. That's my job. If something happens to me, you get back to your car and go get some help. Call the state troopers. You got that?"

Bost swallowed. "Yeah."

"Oh," Watts added, "if I get killed, I expect you to make me look thirty pounds lighter and twenty years younger when you finish your work." There was no time for a reply as the lawmen quickly moved out from his hiding place and toward the grave robbers.

Still contemplating the impossible nature of his friend's final request, Bost watched the sheriff work his way to a fence running along the back of the property and then angle across the cemetery, occasionally dropping down behind large grave makers. Thanks in large part to the cloudy skies, he wasn't spotted.

"Why fill it in?" one of the men asked, his voice carrying across the night to where the funeral director hid.

"So no one knows we took the body," came the quick reply.

Watts, now just twenty feet from the pair, stopped behind a large pine tree, looked back toward Bost for a final time, and after their eyes met, the lawman dipped his head and stepped out into the open. His gun was aimed at the larger of the two men.

"Okay, gentleman, put down the shovels and get your hands up."

With no warning the smaller of the two tossed his spade directly at the sheriff, catching Watts in his ample gut and causing him to slip and fall backward onto the wet ground. With Watts temporarily out of commission, the larger man jumped into the truck and fired it up. As his partner leapt into the bed alongside the coffin, the driver hit the gas. Like a wounded buffalo, the half-ton GMC lurched forward, striking a sixty-year-old granite marker and knocking it flat onto the ground.

"Stop or I'll shoot," Watts hollered, rising to his feet and pulling his pistol to a level position. When the truck speeded up, rolling over the fallen stone, the sheriff let go with four shots, two striking the vehicle's front glass. As the windshield shattered, the pick-up veered to the left and bounced beside a dozen markers before the driver managed to turn right and get back onto the gravel lane. As the vehicle gained traction, Watts shot three more times, knocking out the truck's rear glass and possibly hitting the man in the bed, who fell down beside the coffin. Driven by either fear or an injury, the driver yanked the wheel to the right. Now off the path, the GMC flew into the ditch, causing the coffin to bounce up in the air and crash loudly onto the truck's wooden bed. When the driver shoved the transmission back into first and hit the gas, the vehicle groaned and slowly climbed up the other side of the ditch. As the truck picked up speed, the casket holding Shelton Clark's body slid back in the bed, busted open the tailgate, and teetered for a moment before falling into the mud.

With the law on their tail and fear likely their motivation, the men didn't bother stopping to retrieve what they'd worked so hard to get. Making a hard left, the driver headed the truck down the hill and around a corner. Seconds later the GMC was out of sight behind a large stand of pine trees.

Sensing the fireworks were over, Bost stepped out from behind the tree and jogged over to his friend. He studied Watts, his uniform covered with mud, before asking, "You all right?"

"Yeah," the lawman assured him. "I'm fine." Watts then took a few steps forward, peered into the partially filled grave, and shook his head. "I don't get it."

"I don't either," the funeral director admitted. "I prepared his body for the service, and there was nothing of value in that coffin with him. Not even a class ring."

Watts nodded. "Well, somebody thought there was something there. You sure you don't have any idea as to why this happened?"

"No," Bost assured him. "The casket was a base model, not worth anything to speak of."

Watts pulled his flashlight from his belt and pointed it toward the coffin. He let the beam linger there for a few moments before again splashing light on the partially filled grave. As Bost watched, the lawman moved forward, kicked a bit of mud to one side with his shoe, and grinned. Looking back to his friend he announced, "Well, at least we found your wallet."

CHAPTER 4

Tuesday April 28, 1942
11:30 PM
Outside Drury, Maryland

Becca Bobbs, dressed in dark slacks, a pink cotton blouse, and flats, wasn't happy. Her face framed a mixture of frustration and confusion. Pushing back from her desk, she took another look at what she'd been assured was one of America's most important documents. For the past two days she'd studied this large piece of ancient paper as well as an even older one, the Magna Carta, and her efforts had led to one conclusion . . . they were both perfectly executed forgeries. In fact they were so good they would have fooled almost anyone who didn't have access to the equipment in her lab. The paper was a match and the printing almost perfect, but the ink was a bit off in one small place on the Declaration of Independence. A "the" in the third paragraph didn't look right. On closer inspection it wasn't as dark as it should have been. There was also a tiny break in the letter "e" that was not on any of the photographs she'd studied of the original. That meant all the risks they'd had taken to get the documents were for nothing of any value.

Bobbs, her brow wrinkled, drummed her fingers on her desk. This didn't make sense. Lupino was so sure these two were the real deal that she'd basically staked her life on that fact, and if the woman was to be believed, the documents were being sent to Germany so Hitler could claim he had them. In the crime world this would have been labeled a very elaborate sting, but what was the purpose? Where was the payoff?

As she continued to contemplate the puzzle, she heard the sounds of familiar pumps on the steps behind her. She didn't have to turn around to know Helen Meeker had entered the lab.

"You ready to turn them back over to the White House?" Meeker asked.

"You can take them out to the trashcan if you want." Bobbs got up from her chair and turned to face her guest.

"What?" the team leader asked, her right eyebrow raised indicating disbelief. "The Declaration is a fake. I can point out how I came to that realization if you want. And it stands to reason that if one isn't the real deal, the other isn't either. As my grandfather would have said, someone was trying to bamboozle someone. In this case it appears Alistar Fister was trying to make a monkey out of Hitler."

Meeker, her dark auburn hair pulled back into a ponytail, shook her head. "Hitler does a great job of that all by himself, but Spencer was sure Lupino felt she had the originals."

"I bet she did think they were the real McCoys. But they aren't."

Helen nodded. "Maybe that's why Fister flew the coup rather than making the trip back to Germany. He knew they were fakes. Can you imagine what Hitler would have done if he'd been made to look like a fool?"

"Wouldn't want to be there to watch that."

"So," Meeker said, her voice clearly displaying her irritation, "where are the real documents? I thought we had one-half of our assignment finished."

"Ah, we're back to square one," Bobbs admitted. "We simply don't know." Meeker frowned. "But would you say it's likely whoever gave them to Alistar

Fister still has the real ones?"

"That's the only thing that makes sense. These two documents would probably have been good enough to fool Hitler into thinking he had the real Declaration of Independence and Magna Carta—at least for a while."

"Well, that job is going to be put on hold anyway." "What do you mean?"

"For the moment we've been assigned something new, and this one is right up your alley."

The lab tech grinned. "What have you got?"

Meeker sat in a straight-backed wooden chair and smoothed her gray skirt before bringing her friend up to speed. "Over the last couple of months an American agent, with the help of the underground, found out about a new fuel formula being developed by one of Germany's top research scientists. It's based on the use of hydrogen."

Bobbs nodded. "The theory's been around for years. I mean, we all know there's a limited amount of carbon-based fuel sources. The war has really tightened Germany's supplies. Japan has the same issue. Inside the parts of the earth they control, there's very little crude oil. So if someone developed a hydrogen system that could be used in transportation, it would mean an entire shift in the way a war machine runs. Fuel would no longer be an issue."

"The powers in both London and Washington are well aware of that," Meeker admitted. "So it was essential that our agent Shelton Clark not just get the formula, but also take out the scientist and destroy all his research notes. We got lucky because the man behind this formula was very secretive, always worked alone, and had a habit of sharing nothing until he'd fully tested it."

"I take it Clark was successful."

"Well," Meeker explained, "initially he was. He got into the lab, took photos of all the research and the formula, and put it on microfilm. With the help of a couple of members of the underground, he set up an explosion that took out the facility. The scientist, a man named Kranz—"

"Wilhelm Kranz?" Bobbs interrupted. "Yes."

"He's one of the world's top chemical engineers."

"He *was*," Meeker corrected her. "The underground took

him out." "Shame," Bobbs noted. "He was brilliant."

"Yeah, but he was working for Hitler." Meeker paused and licked her lips before picking up her story. "Anyway, Clark made it back to England via a nighttime crossing of the English Channel. But before he could meet with Russell Strickland, our man in London, and turn over the microfilm, he was shot and killed. Strickland killed one of the attackers and drove the other one off, but the microfilm wasn't on Clark."

"So Germany got it back," Bobbs suggested.

Meeker nodded. "That's what the OSS thought too, so they were trying to track down where it was in Germany. Meanwhile Clark's body was flown to the States, and he was buried in his hometown of Magnolia, Arkansas. Everything the OSS believed was turned upside down last night when someone dug up the grave and tried to steal the coffin."

"Tried?"

"A local lawman stopped them." "Why steal a body?"

"That's what everyone wants to know, and that's why it's being brought here.

You and Dr. Ryan are going to go over it with a fine-tooth comb. There has to be something the OSS missed. I want to know what it is."

"I'll be happy to do what I can," Bobbs assured Meeker. "But I doubt if the OSS could have missed something. Their people are good."

"I'm hoping two days from now, when you've spent some time with the late Mr. Clark, you'll be able to assure me you're better than the OSS."

The ringing of a phone caused the woman to turn her attention from Meeker to her desk. Picking up the receiver from the cradle, Bobbs said, "What do you need?" She listened for a few seconds, nodded, and looked toward her guest.

"Helen, it seems Grace Lupino's been found. Henry wants to know if you'd like to join him in questioning her. He has the Auburn warmed up and ready to go."

Meeker nodded. "Tell him I'm on my way."

CHAPTER 5

Wednesday April 29, 1942
1:10 AM
Washington, D.C.

With Reese behind the wheel, it took just a touch more than an hour to get to the riverfront warehouse district where Grace Lupino was apprehended. As the pair entered a vacant two-story brick building, they found Dr. Cleveland Mills sitting on the corner of an oak roll-top desk, looking down at a cold, wet, frazzled woman appearing more like a storm-soaked cat than a beautiful nightclub singer. As they moved closer Meeker noted the captive's face was bruised, her lips swollen, and her right eye black.

"Trust you had no problem finding the place," Mills said.

"Piece of cake," Reese assured him. "What's the story?"

The doctor looked from the FBI agent to the woman. "Local police found her wandering along the river about four hours ago.

Rather than run from them, she ran toward them. Once in their custody she asked to make a phone call. That call went to the nightclub owner Dick Diamond. Diamond was a little nervous about connecting himself to someone who might put him under the scrutiny of the District Attorney, so he called me. I informed the president as to what was going on, and he advised me to take her off the cops' hands. As the police were still holding her in the general area where she was found, I drove down, picked her up, and brought her to one of the government warehouses along the Potomac. I checked her over physically, gave her some coffee, and waited for you."

"How is she?" Meeker asked.

"Whoever held her worked her over pretty good. I'm guessing some cracked ribs, maybe a broken cheekbone, a couple of lost teeth, but she'll live."

Meeker walked the twenty feet to where Lupino was slumped on an old wooden packing crate. She studied the captive for a few moments then took a place beside her. With Reese and Mills observing from a distance, Meeker began to gently dig for information.

"You don't look like you're feeling too good."

"There's nothing wrong with your vision," Lupino snapped, "but you can't see the half of it. I'm hurting in places I didn't know I had."

"Who did it?" Meeker prodded.

The woman raised her head and drilled Meeker with her dark eyes. "I don't know. Never met them before in my life. But I know the reason they beat me. They wanted what you stole from me. When they were convinced I didn't have them and when that private eye told them another woman had grabbed them from me, they dumped me out here."

She pulled her left arm to a tender spot and winced. "Wished they'd killed me because now he will, and I hate waiting for him to strike."

"Who will?" Meeker probed. "The guy who runs the show." "Fister?"

"No, the man who jerks Fister around like a puppet. Besides, Alistar is probably dead by now."

Meeker looked to Reese and then back to the woman. "Why do you say that?" Pulling her legs up and under her body, Lupino whispered, "The seizures."

"Seizures?"

"Yeah. The stuff they shoot into him to make him strong and that gives him the ability to heal quickly, but it has side effects. In time those side effects will kill him."

"And the seizures are part of that?" Meeker asked, a chill racing down her spine.

Lupino nodded. "They get worse and worse, and evidentially they kill anyone who gets the shots. From what I learned Alistar lasted a lot longer than the ones who went before him. But when we were in Texas, I saw him writhing on the ground, out of his head. I guess I should have shot him and put him out of his misery, but for some sick reason I wanted him to suffer. I wanted him to know what it was like to be completely out of control." She shook her head. "I guess I'm pretty much in that place myself right now."

Meeker pushed off the crate and stood directly in front of Lupino. Reaching forward she gently pulled the woman's chin up until their eyes met.

"Grace, the documents I grabbed from you were fake. The forger's work was good, but they're still worthless."

Her eyes widened then faded. "That's the story of my life—reach for a diamond and end up with glass."

"You thought they were real?" Meeker asked.

Pushing the woman's hand from her chin, Lupino whispered, "Do you think I'd have risked my life for fakes? I thought they'd keep me alive. But nothing's going to do that now." She glanced back to Meeker. "I wish the apartment hadn't burned; there was a red suit there I would have liked to wear in my casket."

Meeker ignored the remark. "Grace, the guy behind all of this—who's he working for?"

She shrugged. "I figured the Germans, but I don't really know. If I did I'd tell you, believe me. I've got nothing to lose."

Meeker pulled her hair from her face, took a final look at a captive who'd been physically, mentally, and spiritually beaten, then turned and walked with long, forceful strides back to the two men.

"You think she's being straight?" Reese asked.

"Yeah." She glanced back at Lupino and studied the woman for a moment before turning to Mills. "Put her in a safe place for a while. Somewhere she can't escape but where no one can get to her either. Deep down she has a real desire to get even with the man she worked for, and while she doesn't have the strength to be much use to us now, we might use her to smoke him out later when she's regained some of her grit and fire.

When that time comes, Dick Diamond will likely be a part of that caper too."

"I'm sure we can come up with a place," Mills said. "But I'm going to be honest.

What she said gives me cause to be concerned about you."

"Yeah," Reese noted. "You have Fister's blood in you."

"You mean the seizures?" Meeker hadn't yet considered that. "What do you think, Doctor? Is that a possibility?"

He nodded. "Depends on a couple of things, and without having more of his blood, I can't be sure about either."

"What are they?" Meeker asked.

Mills looked back at their captive as he spoke. "The reaction Lupino spoke of might be caused by a build-up that happens over time. If that's the case then you'll likely either have no reaction or a perhaps only a small one."

"That's one," Meeker said. "Don't stop now."

The doctor fixed his eyes on hers. "The other might be that your body will come to need more of the stuff."

"Addiction?"

"Yes," Mills admitted. "But as you've had no signs of that so far, I figure that's a long shot as well."

Meeker looked back at their captive. "It does give me something to think about, though, and another reason to find out who's behind this and what they want. So no time to waste. Let's go, Henry."

As they walked back toward the car, Meeker considered the man she'd seen the night Lupino was snatched. Was he the person behind all this? Was he the puppet master who might hold her life in his hands? If only she knew where to find him.

CHAPTER 6

Friday May 1, 1942
12:50 PM
Outside Drury, Maryland

Dr. Spencer Ryan stepped away from the operating table, looked down at the man's body, and frowned. He'd spent the better part of the morning trying to find something, even working through lunch, and for what? He knew little more than he did three hours ago. Shelton Clark's body, stripped of his clothes, was nothing more than a shell without spirit.

"If only you could talk," Ryan whispered. "If only you could point me in the right direction. But that's not going to happen. You're just going to hold out on me."

Sensing he was finished, that he'd done all he could, the doctor reached up to flip off the overhead light. As he did, his hip bumped into the table, causing Clark's left arm to fall off the side of the table and drop toward the floor. Reaching down, Ryan gently grabbed the hand and placed it back on the table. It was then that lighting struck.

"What's this?"

He glanced to a two-inch wide leather band on the man's left wrist. It wasn't a watchband, so what was its purpose? He flipped Clark's hand over and bent closer. There was something crudely inscribed on the back of the bracelet. Moving the overhead light brought a bit more illumination.

Hebrews 11:1.

"That's interesting, even if I have no idea what it means. Just keep talking to me."

The band was tied on Clark's arm with a series of knots. Pulling off his gloves, Ryan went to work untying them. They were too tight to loosen, so there was no way to actually save the band without damaging it. Grabbing a pair of surgical scissors, he snipped at the leather. After four quick cuts the band fell to the side.

"Well, Mr. Clark," the doctor announced while picking up the band, "I see you were a religious man. Beyond the scripture there's a cross tooled into the leather.

Whoever did that work was far more skilled than the person who crudely carved the scriptural note."

Turning the band over on the back side, Ryan noted something written in ink or paint. As was his habit, he read the message out loud as if his patient could hear the words.

"To Spencer from Uncle Sam."

Setting the band back onto the table, the doctor looked at

Clark's arm. There were at least half a dozen small cuts. The largest of these wounds had taken five stitches to close. The band actually covered one that had four stitches. It was obvious that not long before the agent died, he'd seen a bit of hand-to-hand combat. Fortunately none of the injuries had been serious. It was strange the leather band hadn't been cut during the episode, but weird things happen in war.

Stepping back Ryan took a last look at his patient, flipped a sheet over the body, yanked off his surgical apron, exited the room, and climbed the steps up to the old home's main floor. Though he longed to go to the kitchen and grab something to eat, duty forced him to hurry down the hall to the living room where he found Becca Bobbs and Helen Meeker listening to a Mutual Network news broadcast.

Saturday twenty-four British bombers made a daring daylight raid on the seaports in the Netherlands, striking several railroad yards and airfields. The attack caught the Nazi war machine completely by surprise. Not only is the BBC reporting the raid caused significant damage, but not a single British plane was lost in the attack.

Meanwhile in Burma . . .

Ryan looked from the radio to the women. "Sounds like the Allies had a good day yesterday."

"It seems," Meeker replied, her tone reserved and her expression almost disinterested, "the news is always good, and yet the Nazis and Japs aren't throwing up the white flag. So I'm guessing we aren't hearing the whole story." She brushed her hair back over the shoulder of her light blue sweater before continuing. "Did you figure out why anyone would want to steal Shelton Clark's body?"

The good-looking physician took a seat in a high-backed blue Edwardian chair and crossed his legs. "I can assure you the OSS did a very good job with their autopsy. They left no kidney stone unturned." He waited to see if his shop humor struck a chord, and when no laughs followed, he plowed ahead. "I agree with the report written by the British medical examiner. He died from a bullet wound hitting a major artery, though the injury to his stomach would likely have caused him to bleed to death within five or ten minutes. There was nothing in or on the body containing anything that would have had any value."

The doctor glanced over to Meeker, noting her displeasure in his report, and shook his head. "I really wish there was more I could offer. Helen, as I know you're a Christian, I can offer you a bit of comfort."

"How's that?" she asked, her dark blue eyes locking onto his.

"He wore a leather band on his left wrist that had a cross and a Bible verse inscribed into it."

"What was the verse?"

"Hebrew 11:1."

"That's cryptic," Bobbs chimed in. "And it fits our situation."

"What do you mean?" Ryan asked.

Bobbs, wearing a gray skirt and white blouse, pushed off the couch and walked over to the Zenith. After switching off the radio, she turned to face the doctor. "I learned the verse when I was a kid. It says 'Now faith is the substance of things hoped for, the evidence of things not seen.' And that pretty much describes where we are in the case.

We were hoping to discover a lead, and we have nothing. Oh, and as to my report, there was nothing of value in his clothes either."

"So," Meeker noted, "we're drawing a complete blank. But the mere fact that someone wanted the body and was willing to take the risk to dig it up meant they believed there was something there."

"The formula?" Bobbs asked.

"It has to be," Meeker answered. "And that means the Nazis don't have it either." "But where is it?" Ryan asked.

"Russell Strickland, our man in Britain," Bobbs cut in, "went over the beach where Clark died with a fine-tooth comb. There was nothing there. So if it wasn't on the body and not on the beach and the German agents didn't get it, where could it be?"

"Perhaps it's still in Europe," Ryan suggested.

He watched Meeker's blue eyes. They were cold, dark, and almost lifeless. It was as if she'd gone into a trance. After several seconds of silence, she got up from the couch, strolled out of the room and toward the library.

"Where's she going?" the doctor asked.

Bobbs shook her head. "She's coming up with a plan, but she's not going to share anything until she's sure she's on the right track. And as that usually ends up meaning long hours and hard work, I'm going to grab a nap while I can."

Ryan watched Bobbs exit the room. Alone he switched on the radio and crossed over to the window. As the strains of Glen Miller's "Chattanooga Choo Choo" filled the room, he grimaced. Downstairs was a dead man with a secret he was evidently not going to give up, and somewhere not that far away was an evil woman he couldn't shake from his head or heart. Life wasn't supposed to be this complicated.

CHAPTER 7

Saturday, May 2, 1942
10:07 PM
Outside Litchfield, Illinois

Alistar Fister, dressed in dark slacks and a white shirt, sat in an overstuffed green chair, his feet propped up on an ottoman, listening to an episode of *The Whistler* on the radio. Though he was hardly content, he was comfortable killing time in the old farmhouse study. After all, it was much better than either of the fates he faced just a week or two before. Resting his hands on his stomach, he closed his eyes and relaxed. He was just about to punch a ticket to dreamland when his host stomped into the room.

"Don't get too comfortable," the tall man barked. "You'll soon have a job to do."

Slowly opening his eyes, Alistar stared into Bauer's stern face and frowned. "You mean tonight?"

"Not tonight, but I just got notification from Boston that the professor thinks he's found the package we need. So you'll soon be on the trail of something Hitler wants very badly."

Pulling his feet from the ottoman, the younger man eyed his host like a cat sizing up a songbird and smiled. "You mean the Indian woman's body?"

"No guarantees." Bauer eased down onto a wooden side chair. "But it's the best lead Dr. Williams has had so far."

"So," Alistar cut in, "why do you need me?"

"Because our esteemed man of letters is not into grave-robbing. It's against his professional ethic."

"Well," Alistar cracked, "based on the botched job your guys did trying to steal that OSS agent's body, it doesn't appear our team is too good at it either. I'm betting Hitler was none too pleased with that blunder."

"He doesn't know about it," Bauer admitted. "In fact, he believes we examined the body and it revealed nothing. As the OSS is a top-flight organization with some of the best minds in the world, they would have discovered what the agent had before they shipped the body home. So I'm sure we would have found nothing anyway. Thus it appears the formula is lost."

"Why did the Germans want the man's body?" Alistar asked. "I know our purpose in digging up the Indian's grave, but what about them?"

"They figured he must have swallowed the micro film to smuggle it back to England," Bauer explained. "That's why the agents cut open his stomach when they attacked him. But as they found nothing that night on the beach and the OSS found nothing in their autopsy, it all must have been a charade."

"A charade?"

"Yes. The agent must have passed the formula on to someone else, and neither the Germans nor the Allies know who it is."

"And you don't either?" Alistar grinned. "I'm shocked. I thought only God knew more than you."

"No, I don't know," Bauer snapped, "and I don't care. As I've told you, the outcome of the war isn't important; it's making money and gaining power during the war

that matters. And that's why you're going to oversee this operation of finding the Caddo woman's body."

"When?"

"Not for a few days. First I want you to meet with Dr. Williams, have him take you to the spot and get a feel for things. Find out what day and what time will be best for doing this and not attracting any suspicion. Once you figure it out, contact me and I'll assign you two men who'll do the dirty work."

"When do I leave?"

"Monday. You'll meet Williams at his home and then go down to Arkansas where he believes the woman is buried. Before then I'll give you another dose of my formula and do some testing. I don't want you having a seizure while you're gone."

"Glad you're so concerned about me."

Bauer glared at his guest, shook his head in disgust, then got up and left the room.

As he did, Alistar laughed. He'd do what Bauer wanted; after all, it was his ticket to staying alive. But just maybe this trek would also give him another option. If by some chance they did find the woman, and there was a map and the water that map led them to did have some type of restorative power, then perhaps he could end Bauer's reign over him—and maybe his life too. That was something that would bring a lifetime of sweet dreams.

CHAPTER 8

Sunday, May 3, 1942
9:31 AM
Washington, D.C.

Getting into the oval office was never easy. To actually get to the president you f i r s t had to been seen by several people. Thus, for a person the world thought was dead to have a face-to-face conversation with FDR was all but impossible. For Helen Meeker there was only one path to see the most powerful man in the world, and Dr. Cleveland Mills provided it. The fact she'd been able to convince Mills was more a testament to his big heart than her logic. The physician seemed to believe the meeting would bear no fruit, but it would be good for both Meeker and Roosevelt to see each other again. He even told the woman as they drove to the White House, "In times like these, when the world is literally falling apart, renewing friendships and having actual eye contact is more important than ever."

"What is it?" the president called out in response to a hand rapping on his open office door.

"It's time for me to do a bit of medical work," Mills announced, a grin covering his round face.

The president looked past the doctor to a gray-headed woman dressed in a white nurse's uniform. Her thick glasses hinted at her vision issues, and the padding around her midsection likely assured the nation's leader the woman wasn't inclined toward much exercise either. As FDR frowned in disgust, Meeker saw no glimmer of recognition in his eyes. The president had been fooled. There was a touch of satisfaction in that. No one pulled the wool over this man's eyes too often.

"I had a physical two weeks ago," the president grumbled as his gaze went from the nurse to the doctor. "I feel fine."

"I'm sure you do," Mills replied as he closed the door and locked it. "But you still need to give us a few minutes of your time."

"Us?" the president asked, moving his eyes from his doctor back to the nurse. "Shouldn't you both be in church? After all, it's Sunday morning. Go say a prayer for me, but for heaven's sake leave me alone. I get fussed over enough through the week without having my weekends messed up by quacks."

Ignoring the scolding Meeker smiled, slowly pulled the glasses from her nose, and approached FDR's desk. She let him study her until she finally noted a sly smile.

"You always have been a crafty gal," the president announced. "But I'm not sure this is one of your brightest stunts."

"I needed to see you," she explained. "There's a matter we need to discuss, and the phone wasn't going to cut it. I also knew Alison or Dr. Mills couldn't fully share what I needed to say."

"What you actually mean," he corrected her, "is that your idea is too outlandish for them to go along with."

"I don't know about that," she lied.

"It is that important?" His eyebrows arched above the top of his wire-rimmed glasses.

"Yes," she assured him.

"Then take a seat and spill it. But I still think you need to be in church. We need prayer as much as we need tanks right now. At least, that's what I've been told by the Navy Chaplain." He waved his hand. "What does a navy man know about tanks anyway?"

As Mills retired to a chair beside a table on the far side of the room, Meeker eased down into one right in front of the president's desk. Crossing her left white-stocking clad leg over her right knee, she got directly to the point.

"I need a ticket punched." "To where?"

"Behind enemy lines in Europe."

"That's not a travel destination right now—at least not for you. If you remember, I promised your father I'd look out for you."

"And you've done a good job," Meeker quickly replied, "but I promised I would serve you and the interests of this country. I've got a mission I need to complete, and it just happens to be in Germany."

Roosevelt picked up an already lit cigarette from where it rested in an overflowing ashtray and took a deep draw. After exhaling and watching the smoke hover in the air, he glanced back to the woman. "I don't remember assigning you anything that involved overseas travel."

"In a way you did," she argued. "You gave us the job of trying to figure out why someone would want to steal Shelton Clark's body."

"And," FDR shot back, "your sister tells me you came up empty. I believe that was your report."

"The body offered nothing," Meeker agreed, "but that means the formula must still be out there. And the body being removed from the grave pretty much assures us the Nazis don't know where it is."

FDR nodded. "The OSS and FBI have given me reports that say that as well. So what makes you think you know where this formula is when the top spies on both sides are stumped?"

"Well," Helen said, "if the agent didn't have the formula, then he must have sensed a trap and given it to the man or men he was with. Who did he work with? Who got him across the English Channel?"

The president shook his head. "That's classified."

"I'm dead," she shot back. "You even sent flowers to my funeral. I think you can share pretty much anything with a ghost. After all, only a few people believe in us."

He sighed. "Fine. I guess it won't hurt to tell a spook. The contact was with a man everyone knows as The Snake. Even I don't know his real identity, and the only way to actually contact him is through a man named Strickland in London."

"Russell Strickland?"

"You know the name, I see."

"He works with the OSS and is our liaison with the underground." "You get a gold star," the president quipped.

"I need to meet with The Snake."

"Helen, he's behind enemy lines. And the *behind* element in that statement means we aren't there. I don't plan on sending you anywhere we aren't."

"Actually," Meeker acknowledged with a sly grin, "you need to rethink that."

"It's suicide," the president replied. "If I sent you, I'd be the one responsible." "You got Shelton Clark in there," she shot back.

"He was trained for the mission. He speaks four different languages. You don't even speak German."

"Becca Bobbs does," Meeker countered, "and she'll be going with me." "Two women?" The president laughed. "You expect me to drop two women behind enemy lines so you can get an interview with a man whose identity is the most closely guarded secret of the war. Young lady, there are some things I won't do even for you."

Meeker didn't back down. Instead she leaned toward the president and pushed forward with another question. "Does the formula really exist?"

"From what we know," the president assured her, "we believe

it does." "And if the Nazis find it and put it into use?"

"It changes the dynamic of the war," he admitted. "Oh, I still think we'll win. I believed that even before we got into the war. But if the Nazis put the formula into use, it'll cost a lot more lives and take us a lot longer to claim victory."

"Let me see," Meeker noted. "As I remember it, you're sixty-three." "Sixty-four," he corrected her.

"And you want to actually live to see the end of the war," she teased. "Is that

right?"

"Helen, where are going with this?"

She smiled. "If the war lasts too long, you might not see us raise the American flag over Berlin. So you need to let me find that formula for you so things don't drag out too long."

FDR frowned. "Young lady, you are not being funny."

"Losing a lot more lives," she pointed out, "is no laughing matter either. If my theory is right about finding the formula, then the risk will be more than worth it. Besides, as Becca and I are supposedly dead, the Nazis can't kill us anyway."

"If you're trying to be logical, you're failing. Besides, what makes you believe you can do something the S.S. and the OSS can't?"

"A hunch."

"You want to risk your life on a hunch?"

"I saved you and Churchill by playing a hunch. I can point out others that have panned out as well."

He sighed again. "I don't guess it will hurt me to listen to what's on your mind. In fact, it might be the only way for me to get you out of my office so I can do some work."

Meeker grinned. "All you have to do is let me get to this Snake and find out what he knows. Let me meet with him face-to-face. Drop us in, and then let the underground smuggle us back to Britain. It's done all the time."

"Helen, Strickland has already contacted The Snake and he knows nothing that can help us."

"Just give me the chance."

"I won't risk your life for the formula."

"Is my life more important than a million civilians or a few hundred thousand men in uniform?"

"Of course not," FDR admitted.

"Then arrange for the trip. Besides, Clay's contacts tell me the Germans got their hands on some of the official plates needed to print real English money. Clay also said the underground managed to retrieve them, and now someone needs to pick them up." She leaned closer. "And let me remind you of something the British have already proven."

"What's that?"

"Attractive women not only make better spies but draw less attention than male agents. Men talk to us, but they never seem to notice what we're really doing. Thanks to our physical charms, Becca and I can get in and out and have a lot better chance of surviving than a man would. And I have a hunch The Snake would trust us more as well."

"It's stupid," FDR argued. "There's no real purpose. There's nothing you can do that our existing teams can't."

Meeker smiled. "Then you'd better arrest me and put me in a Federal Prison because even if you don't set things up, I'll find a way to get behind enemy lines and to The Snake. And you know as well as I do that I'll make good on my promise."

Roosevelt put his cigarette holder between his lips and locked his eyes onto his guest. For three full minutes he stared at her without even blinking. Shaking his head he finally looked away. As he did he made a suggestion. "Is there a certain prison you want to call home, or do I get to pick out your next address?"

"You wouldn't dare!"

"I'd like to," he assured her then grinned. "If you go in the outfit you're wearing now, the Germans will likely not even notice you and The Snake will surely run the other direction."

"We need to do this quickly," Meeker said with a smile.

"If you get captured," FDR warned, "I'll find a way to haunt you." "Is that a promise or a threat?"

"Okay, I'll pull the strings," the president announced, "but there's one requirement."

"What's that?"

"Henry Reese goes with you."

"We don't need Henry," she argued.

"Then you don't go. Last time I looked I ran this country, not you." He snapped his fingers and looked over to Mills. "What's that new female comic book hero?"

"Wonder Woman?" the doctor replied.

"Yeah," the president said with a shake of his head. "Helen, you are no Wonder Woman, so I'm going to send the closest thing I have to Superman with you. Are you going to play by my rules, or do you want me to send you to the Federal Pen?"

"I'll play," she grumbled.

"Okay, get back to your headquarters and we'll arrange a flight to London. Once you're there Russell Strickland will take over the arrangements and do whatever he needs to do to get you to The Snake."

"Thank you, sir," Meeker said as she stood up.

"Get out of here before I change my mind," he barked. "And never wear that ridiculous outfit again."

CHAPTER 9

Friday, May 8, 1942
2:15 AM
Petit Jean Mountain, Arkansas

As Professor Warren Williams and Alistar Fister looked on from the rocks at the top of the Ozark mountain peak, two of Bauer's mute hired men used shovels to dig down into the soil just below the top of the bluff. Thick clouds hid the half moon, so no one could spot their nefarious actions.

"We drew a break with the cloud cover," Williams noted.

"We didn't get lucky." Alistar corrected the older man. "I noted they were predicting rain tonight. If this weather had come a day earlier, we'd have done it then." He paused, glanced back to where the men were digging, and asked, "So you believe Kawutz is buried there?"

"From what the old woman in Conway told me," Williams replied, "this is where the grave has to be."

"But the legends say this is the burial spot of the Frenchwoman who disguised herself as a cabin boy to make the trip to the New World."

"Let me explain something to you," Williams said, his tone much like that of a teacher mentoring a student. "Santa Claus is a legend, while St. Nicholas was the real deal. The former was based on the latter, but the latter is nothing more than fantasy. Santa does not live at the North Pole or have a team of reindeer, but sixteen centuries ago the red-robed Nicholas actually did give presents to children. So don't get fact and fiction confused, no matter how appealing fiction can be."

"And what does that have to do with this?"

Williams checked on the workers' progress then glanced back over his shoulder from the dirt road to the overlook, no doubt checking to confirm they were still alone before continuing his lecture. "My research, as I told you when we first met, shows there was no Petit Jean who came to America. Maybe the Frenchmen did bury something in this place, but I'm sure it wasn't a French woman."

"So that's all you to have to go on that claims this as being the place the Indian was buried?" Alistar's sarcastic tone proved he was completely unimpressed with the old man's reasoning.

"The old woman told me Kawutz's spirit walks the government land that overlooks the river. I did my homework and searched through scores of documents. I drove up and down the Arkansas River, and this is the only place that seemed to fit. And what better place to hide a body than in a grave where a non-existent legend was supposedly laid to rest? I mean, who would look for it there?" Williams glanced over the bluff at the Arkansas River bottom far below. "This has to be the place. I feel sure we'll find Kawutz today, and with her body will be the map we need to locate the Fountain of Youth."

Alistar, trying to maintain his false identity as the Scottish antiquities expert, considered the older man's hopeful story before turning his attention back to the workers. In an hour they had dug down about five feet. How deep would the Indians have placed the body?

"Dr. Williams."

"Yes."

"You seem to put a great deal of stock in the reality of the Fountain of Youth."

The professor looked from the river to the man he believed was sponsoring his work. After folding his arms over this chest, he spoke in tones so hushed it seemed as if he actually believed the dead Caddo woman might be able to overhear him. "Did you know there's a drug in use by the American military to cure disease that was almost always fatal just five years ago?"

"No," Alistar admitted.

"A Frenchman," Williams explained, "Rene Dubos, was one of the first to develop this drug. The term for the medicine is antibiotic. A new version of this antibiotic, penicillin, is being used by the army right now." He paused as if searching for a way to fully explain his point then continued. "Are you a fan of motion pictures?"

"I go to the movies from time to time."

"In 1937 Jean Harlow was the most popular actress on this planet. She contracted the flu and it settled in her kidneys. In just days this vibrant woman was dead at the age of twenty-six. Five years ago her case was deemed hopeless. Today an antibiotic would likely have put her back on her feet and making movies within a week."

"Professor, that's all well and good, but it doesn't answer my question." "Actually it does." Williams corrected the younger man. "There are hundreds of

things, such as airplanes or even aspirin, that would have been considered fantasy a century ago and we now take for granted. Therefore who's to say there isn't a natural spring with a chemical that might have curative powers or even the ability to prolong life?"

Alistar raised his eyebrows. "You believe that?"

The older man shrugged. "It wasn't too long ago that learned men didn't believe in dinosaurs, but that doesn't mean they didn't exist. My point is this. I will not rule out that Kawutz didn't live for centuries until I've been to the well and tested the water."

Williams grinned. "While I want to believe the legend is actually fact, what my brain tells me is that what we'll find will be nothing more than a hidden spring with the same water we drink every day. And I also fear the woman I've researched for so many years is actually a dozen or more women that oral history paints as one. It all goes back to separating fact from fiction or reality from legend."

Alistar considered the words as he once more walked over the large rocky outcroppings on the side of the mountain. Glancing down at the workers, he noted they had tossed their shovels to one side and were busy sweeping away dirt from the top of what appeared to be an oblong wooden box.

"Professor, I think we have something."

As the old man scrambled to the top of the boulder and glanced down the thirty feet to where a lantern illuminated what was at the bottom of the hole, he smiled. "My hunch was right. The old woman gave me just enough information to find what we were looking for."

"How do you know it's not the Frenchwoman?" Alistar asked. "Wouldn't they have made a casket for her?"

"It's easy to see, even from here, that the coffin is of the design used early in this century," Williams explained. "Tell them to lift it out. You and I need to open it up and see what's inside."

"Men," Alistar called out, "pull that thing out of the hole. We'll climb down and join you."

With an openly excited and surprisingly agile Williams leading the way, the two wound down a rocky, narrow trail that meandered more than a hundred yards along the rocky bluff, carefully maneuvering along cliffs that dropped several hundred feet. Just as they arrived, the workers pulled the hardwood box out of the ground and set it beside the grave.

"Let me see that hammer," Williams ordered, his impatience

showing. After it was handed to him, the professor hurriedly began to pry the top edge of the casket. As a long line of three-inch nails secured it, the task was anything but quick or easy. With the mute workers looking at the older man, Alistar turned his attention from the energized professor to the hole. The lantern's glow revealed something else was hidden there.

Dropping down into what had been a grave, he fell to his knees and studied a fist-sized opening in the four-inch thick flat rock lining the place where the coffin had rested.

"Professor," Alistar called out, "there appears to be a wooden chest of some kind hidden below a large flat rock."

Not even pausing with his efforts to open the casket, a breathless Williams called out, "Likely filled with gold or silver. I've long believed the French explorers must have buried treasure they accumulated on their trip somewhere. It makes sense they'd invent the story of the dead woman's grave as a way of keeping people from knowing about their loot."

Alistar grinned. "We need to take this stuff with us."

"Maybe another time," Williams suggested. "It would be far too heavy for us to take now. We'd need a block and tackle to get it up to the top of the mountain, or we'd have to carry it out piece by piece. At this moment we have neither the equipment nor the time."

"But—"

"No buts," the professor continued. "We know where it is, and no one is looking for it. We'll put this box back in the ground when we leave, cover it up, make it look as though no one has been here, and then you can come back later to get what you found." He paused, wiped sweat from his brow, and laughed. "Okay, this thing is about to come open."

Scrambling out of the hole, Alistar grabbed the lantern, took a spot at the foot of the coffin, and watched wide-eyed as Williams pushed the lid to one side. He was shocked at what the dim light revealed. "She looks like she's asleep," Alistar announced. "She doesn't look any different than she did in her photo."

Williams leaned closer to the body and smiled. "I've never seen a body so well prepared that it didn't deteriorate a bit. I wonder what they used to preserve her."

As the amazed old man continued to hover over the dead woman's face, Alistar asked the question that was most important to both himself and Bauer. "Professor, what about the map?"

Williams, his eyes never leaving the woman's face, pointed to Kawutz's right hand. "I'm betting that's what she's holding." Standing upright the professor glanced at the luminous dial on his watch. "We have rope and blankets in the car." He looked at Alistar, his tone suddenly assertive and urgent. "Grab them and throw them down here. While you do that, I'll get the body and everything else out of the casket. Then we'll put the lid back on the box, drop it into the grave, cover it up, and make it appear like we've never been here. I can't emphasize this enough; we have to leave this place making sure nothing looks disturbed."

As the older man went to work on Kawutz, Alistar hurried back up the trial and to Williams' Packard station wagon they'd brought on their trip. After retrieving the requested items, he hurried over to the boulders and looked down to the gravesite. Things were now moving quickly. The two workers already had the box back in the ground and were filling the hole.

"Toss the stuff down," Williams ordered. "I'll fix a gurney, wrap her in it, and we can use the ropes to lift her straight up. You just stay there. I'll need your muscle."

"Are you sure we have the map?" Alistar asked as he dropped the materials to the professor.

"Don't worry about it," the old man called out. "I've checked. It's here, and I should be able to decipher it back at my office. Now let's get everything taken care of and this place cleaned up."

Thirty minutes later, after a final inspection to make sure the graveside appeared as it did when they arrived, Williams glanced at his partner in crime. "Okay. It looks

perfect. And if it rains tonight, it'll wash away whatever signs of our visit I might have missed."

Alistar turned to the two men waiting by a 1934 Chevy sedan. "You can leave." With their pockets lined with the cash they'd received for their labors, the mute workers didn't linger. Getting into their car, they started the engine, turned left, and headed down the dirt road into the river valley. After the duo's departure, Alistar and Williams, their cargo hidden under several blankets, took a final look at the dramatic view from the mountaintop.

"We did it," the weary but still excited professor announced as he looked toward the younger man. "But without your organization's support, this never would have happened."

"Dr. Williams, it's just the first step. We now have to find the fountain."

"We will," the man boldly proclaimed. "But sadly, it will likely be just another Ozark spring."

Saying no more, the professor turned, walked over to the passenger side of the large car, opened the door, and slid in. As he shut the door, a few sprinkles of rain began to fall.

Taking a final look at the Arkansas River Valley, a smiling Alistar moved to the driver's side of the car. Just before he pulled the door handle, he heard a noise from the side of the ridge. Looking a hundred feet to his left, he noted half a dozen birds fly out of an oak tree. Suddenly a frown replaced his smile. What had spooked them? As the rain picked up, his eyes focused on the tree. Though he saw nothing, he felt as if he were being watched. Could there be someone else here, or was the ghost of the Indian woman upset that her grave had been disturbed and her body taken? A bit unnerved and suddenly apprehensive, Alistar opened the door, jumped into the station wagon, started the powerful straight-eight motor, and hurriedly drove away from the mountaintop.

CHAPTER IO

Friday May 8, 1942
8:15 AM
Somewhere over the Atlantic

Helen Meeker's team caught a ride with a Royal Air Force ferry group taking new American-built planes from the United States to Britain. While the Consolidated B-24 Liberator was anything but comfortable, it did offer the fastest way of getting from America to London, and travelling over the ocean in this metal bird was much safer than riding the plane on its future missions over Germany. Odds were pretty long against the bomber's crew surviving very many runs against the Nazi Luftwaffe. The northern route took the trio first to Newfoundland and then Iceland before making the final jump to an English air base located just outside London.

Meeker, dressed in an RAF flight suit a couple of sizes too large for her frame, sat on the floor and glanced to her right to check on her female team member. A seemingly unconcerned Becca Bobbs was curled up in a sleeping bag and lost on a trip to dreamland. To the blonde, every day was a new adventure to be relished, and she never seemed to worry about the outcome. In her world life was to be lived in the moment.

As Henry Reese walked back from the cockpit, Meeker's eyes shifted to the other member of the mission. His flight suit fit as if it had been designed for his muscular frame and reminded her once more of what a handsome man he was. After he dropped down on the floor to her right, he leaned close enough to be heard over the engine's roar. "We have about another hour and we'll be on the ground."

That was the best news she'd heard since leaving their headquarters. After more than twenty-four hours with the bomber shaking her body like a puppy shook a ragdoll, she was more than ready to feel the earth beneath her feet. She also longed for a real bed and some peace and quiet. Unlike Bobbs, Meeker couldn't sleep anywhere she laid down.

Reese leaned close again. "You ever wish you were someplace else doing something much different?"

Meeker looked at Reese and shrugged. Where was he going? What was he thinking? "Like where?"

"Maybe a lake in Canada," he suggested, "or on the rollercoaster at Coney Island."

"I don't really think about stuff like that," she admitted. "I just focus on what's happening now."

"Helen, our jobs depend upon pain and suffering. Even before the war we were called in only when someone had experienced a tragic loss. Now it's even worse. Death haunts some; it lives with us. In fact, we eagerly open the door and let it in. It's what fuels our passion and gives us a reason to live. We're only needed because there's evil and suffering in the world."

Though she only occasionally thought about it before this moment, Reese was right. People had to get hurt for her to have a reason to work, but at this moment that fact didn't bother her like it did her male partner. Meeker shrugged again. "Henry, someone has to do it."

"Why you? Most women your age are at home; they have a couple of kids, and they don't relish looking at a dead body. They live for hearing a child's first words or seeing a baby's first steps."

She shook her head. "That's not for me right now. You see, I need to—" He cut her off. "To show the world you're as good as any man."

Meeker's defenses went into overdrive. "I want those things too, you know. I want to have children, I want a husband, and I want a home with a picket fence, but—"

He interrupted her again. "But you want something else much more."

"What's that?" she demanded. "If you're so smart and know me so well, what is it?"

"You want to best every man on earth first. That kind of thinking will kill you, Helen."

She frowned and stubbornly looked back across the plane.

Men were so narrow- minded, especially Henry. How could he possibly bring this up now? There was a war going on, and everyone had to pull their weight and do their part. The British women had been doing men's work for a couple of years now. Why had the president demanded they bring him along?

"Helen," he continued, "you're good. No, you're a lot better than good; you're amazing. But I wonder if what you're giving up to prove that you're a man's equal isn't costing you more than you know." His eyes locked onto hers. "Don't you want to love and be loved? Don't you want to share your heart and soul with someone who loves you?"

"That sounds a lot like a proposal."

He shook his head. "It's not, but that doesn't mean I don't have feelings for you. Since the first time I kissed you . . . Do you remember that kiss? We were working on the case where you got that yellow Packard. Well, ever since that time I've longed for more than just a working relationship between us. From the very beginning I knew there wasn't another woman in the world like you. But I also knew you were driven by a goal you can't really achieve. Worse yet, your mission to reach that goal will never end. It can't because there'll always be another man you have to show up and another thing you have to prove."

Pushing off the floor she angrily stomped across the plane and looked out a gun sight. Cloud cover prevented her from seeing the ocean, but she knew it was there. There was also a cloud covering her future. She didn't know what direction she'd go or how things would work out, but she was sure of one thing:

Henry was likely the only man who would ever understand her and be strong enough to love her. Deep down, in places where she wouldn't allow herself to go, she likely had love stored up for him too. But she didn't want to think about that now.

Meeker sensed Reese walk up behind her. A moment later she smelled his aftershave as he leaned close to her ear.

"I'm sorry, Helen. I shouldn't have said what I said. I have no right to judge you or dictate how you live your life."

She turned to face him. "In another time and another place, when we weren't at war and life was sure and steady, maybe I could surrender to the world you painted with your words. It's appealing. I even dream about it at night. But I can't give into those feelings when people are dying and mad men are racing to control the world."

He smiled. "I know that." He paused, ran his finger over her cheek, "But I need to know something anyway."

"What's that?"

"Do you love me?"

He wasn't letting her off easy. In fact he was pressing in ways she'd never been pressed before, and she'd never felt so uncomfortable.

"I might," she finally admitted just loud enough to be heard over the engines. "I know I care more about you than I do anyone else. But with the war going on, my mind isn't sure of much of anything other than a need to do something more than be a regular woman. I can't separate my feelings from my mission."

"For now that'll do," he assured her. "Besides, with you

taking on the Nazis, the war can't last long. They don't have a chance against Helen Meeker. After you kick Hitler in the rear, we'll have time to make a few dreams come true."

"Yeah," she whispered.

As Meeker watched, Reese moved to a spot along the far wall and sank back to the floor, closed his eyes, and tried to grab a bit of sleep. Maybe it was a good thing the president demanded this man come along. Right now she couldn't begin to imagine a mission without her partner by her side, and as she looked into her future, she saw him there as well.

CHAPTER II

Saturday, May 9, 1942
8:15 PM
Thirty miles outside Berlin, Germany

After flying from New York to London and meeting OSS agent Russell Strickland, Reese, Bobbs, and Meeker boarded a small airplane and used the cover of night to cross the channel to Europe. The craft, piloted by an RAF pilot named Andrew St. John, stayed low, using a path taking it only over rural areas before setting down in a field less than thirty miles from the nerve center of the Nazi war effort. After the quartet disembarked, they pushed the plane into a barn, hid it behind bales of hay, and closed the door. For a half-hour the four nervously leaned against the outside barn wall and waited in the shadows. It was just before nine when a Mercedes sedan turned off the road and stopped. A woman wearing a long coat and hat stepped out of the vehicle. After carefully scanning the area, she reached into her pocket, pulled out a white handkerchief, and waved it above her head. As a response, Meeker, still hidden by the building's shadows, turned on a flashlight for a second and then shut it off. The visitor then lowered her arm down, slid back into the black car, and flashed the lights.

"That's our ride," Meeker announced. "And right on time," Reese added.

Meeker had experienced half a dozen different situations where her life was on the line, but this was different. Working for the president was not going to offer an out this time. She was on foreign soil, up against a ruthless enemy that was all around her.

And though she knew hundreds of agents used this method to enter, gain information, and exit Europe, there were many others who didn't come home. They died or were captured by the Nazis. Some were even betrayed by members of the underground. Fear was suddenly so thick and close she could smell it, and for a second she yearned for the normal life Reese had spoken of on the flight over.

Taking a deep breath, she looked at her companions. Though she was primed for action, Bobbs displayed no fear or apprehension. She seemed relaxed, her eyes taking in the scene around her as if she were on a vacation. The other member of the party was the polar opposite.

Henry Reese's jaw was set, his expression grim, almost mournful, his body stiff, his hand on his gun and his eyes darting across the landscape as if trying to keep up with a car race. For all intent he appeared to be a man going to his own funeral.

"You okay, Henry?" Meeker asked.

"Fine," he replied, never taking his gaze from the road that ran along the property. "Time to go?" Bobbs asked, her enthusiastic tone almost childlike.

Meeker grinned. "Becca, you don't need to act as though this is a trip to the circus. I don't think anyone is going to be selling popcorn or cotton candy."

"Sorry," the woman whispered. "It's just that I've never felt more alive. There's something about being out on a limb that brings a huge rush."

"Living on the edge is overrated," Reese warned. "In situations like this death is hovering around every corner. So don't get so caught up in the moment you lose your wits."

"But, Henry," Meeker dryly noted, "you're always complaining about the FBI not letting you join the Marines. You gripe that Hoover is forcing you to stay thousands of miles from the war. Well, right now you're far deeper in Germany than anyone in the American military. So you have your wish. Or was it just the uniform you wanted?"

The FBI agent shrugged. "I guess I need to be careful what I pray for." After forcing a nervous smile, he added, "But you're right. I've spent the last few months wanting to be exactly where we are tonight. I wanted to be taking on the Nazis up close and personal. I wanted to feel like I was doing something for the war effort."

"And you are," Meeker assured him. "Don't forget, I'm the

one who made your wish come true. So be sure and thank me when you get the chance." Her eyes caught his as he nodded.

"I'm guessing by thanks you mean flowers and dinner?" "And diamonds," Meeker added.

"Fat chance," Reese grumbled.

"Don't bother," Meeker quipped. "I wouldn't want to put you out. Besides, you're just along for the ride. Becca and I could have handled this on our own."

"Listen to the brave woman," Reese said with a frown.

Meeker grinned. "I believe our ride is waiting. I'm calling shotgun."

"Hey," Bobbs asked, "before we leave we need to know what time our ride back to England is leaving."

"We need to get out of here by one," St. John explained. "My orders won't allow me to wait any longer than that. There's fuel in the barn. While you're gone I'll gas up."

"We got it," Meeker assured him as she looked at her watch. "And don't worry; I've never been late for a flight yet."

As the British pilot stayed behind, the trio of Americans hurriedly crossed the meadow to the vehicle. When they arrived the driver stepped out and said, "Browns."

"St. Louis," Meeker replied. She was now close enough to see their contact was a tall, thin blonde dressed in a long gray coat and hat.

"Chicago," the woman announced. "Cubs," Meeker answered.

"Call me Maria," the driver announced in English tinged

with a heavy Germanic accent. "Let's get moving. The Snake is on a mission about ten kilometers up the road. He'll meet with you briefly when he and his team are finished."

"Does he have the plates?" Reese asked.

"Actually," Maria replied, as she stepped back in the car, "I have them. They're resting on the backseat."

Once they were in the car and the doors had been shut, the Mercedes made a large circle in the field and pulled out of the gate. As Maria guided the sedan onto the rural road, Meeker glanced toward the backseat and spied Reese slipping the plates into his inside pocket.

"Don't lose those," Meeker cautioned. "Those things'll help keep me in the president's good graces."

Reese grinned. "And we wouldn't want that to change."

Bobbs, still looking like a teen on a trip to a carnival, glanced out the window into a wooded area beyond an ancient stone wall. "What's The Snake's mission?"

The driver, her eyes catching Bobbs' in the review mirror, smiled. "There's a meeting in the town hall of a village up the road tonight. Those gathered are supposed to review plans for some kind of new weapon in development."

"So this is The Snake's party?" Reese asked.

"Let's say he's not on the guest list," Maria explained. "But it's something he doesn't feel he can miss. After all, Himmler will be there, and The Snake is hoping it all ends with a rather large bang."

"What do we do?" Meeker asked.

The woman smiled. "You stay out of the way. When everything is set, he'll see you. I'm taking you to a safe house."

Confident that a plan was in place, the four rode in silence until they noted a large German troop truck parked beside the road. Standing beside it were a half-dozen men dressed in Nazi uniforms.

"This isn't right," Maria noted, her voice showing concern. "The meeting is up the road at a small farm house. Nothing should be going on here."

Meeker reached into her pocket and found her Colt. As her finger eased over the trigger she said, "I hope those are your guys dressed up for Halloween."

"No," Maria whispered, "and there are likely more of them within a stone's throw. Let me handle this. If any of you shoot, we'll all be dead before we can get out of the car. If there's just some small party at this farm, likely a few officers and their wives, I'm sure they'll let us pass."

"And if not?" Reese asked.

There was no time for an answer.

When two soldiers stepped out in the road, Maria slowed to a stop. She waited as one moved over to the driver's window and glanced in. He studied them for a few seconds, smiled, and asked a question. As Maria answered, Meeker glanced toward the backseat. Bobbs, her face showing concern for the first time, was listening intently to the conversation. Beside her Reese was nervously drumming his fingers on the car seat.

"Danke," Maria said at the end of the exchange, and the

soldier backed away from the door. Pushing the car into first, she pulled away.

"Are we clear?" Meeker asked.

"The meeting was moved here earlier today. It seems the other location couldn't hold all the people that were coming. And rather than being a strategy session, it seems this has become some kind of celebration." She paused and cut a quick glance at Helen. "We're invited."

"What do you mean?" Meeker asked.

Bobbs leaned forward and explained. "The men thought we were the ladies being brought in for tonight's entertainment."

"That's right," Maria said.

"What does that make me?" Reese asked. "Our employer," Bobbs said.

"We're not dressed for this part," Meeker pointed out. "Evidently," Maria said, "our wardrobe arrived earlier in the day."

As the Mercedes joined a dozen other cars in front of the two-story white stone mansion, Meeker noted German soldiers on all sides. They couldn't simply get out of the car and walk away. There would be no easy escape.

"What do we do?" Bobbs asked, her expression a mixture of confusion and fear. "Whatever it takes to get out alive," Maria answered.

Meeker nodded. But what would that be? And where was The Snake?

CHAPTER 12

Saturday May 9, 1942
10:23 PM
Thirty miles outside Berlin, Germany

The place they'd been taken was more of a suite than a bedroom. With its lavish furniture, beautiful paintings, ornate mirrors, and thick rugs, it dripped of old money. On the large red-velvet-covered bed were stacks of dresses, all new and anything but modest. They might have been brought in from one of Berlin's finest lady's shops or perhaps stolen from a Paris boutique. Whoever designed them likely didn't have family gatherings in mind.

As Meeker finished slipping into the slinky, formfitting, low-cut, floor-length light blue gown, she glanced toward Bobbs. Her friend was zipping up a red number of a similar style.

"The front sure looks like the back," Bobbs noted.

"Mine too," Meeker agreed. "But if I turn it around, it's even worse."

"Got a plan?" Bobbs tried to adjust the dress to cover more of her pale flesh.

"I saw enough when they escorted us in," Meeker explained, "to realize that a lot of the top-ranking officers in the Luftwaffe are here tonight. It looks like a New Year's Eve party. Whatever we walked into is much bigger than anything we could have expected." She waltzed over to the window and looked down to the front drive. At least twenty cars were now parked there. Beside one of them stood Henry Reese, but it seemed

most of the officers that had earlier been mingling on the grounds had moved inside the large home.

As Meeker turned she watched Bobbs grab a brush and go to work on her hair.

After several strokes she glanced at her friend and asked, "Where did Maria go?"

"She slipped into a black dress and walked out the door and down the stairs with a short, fat officer." Meeker frowned. "Becca, do you realize that by entertainers they don't expect us to actually sing or dance?"

"Yeah," Bobbs said. "I figured that out. Did you see the way they ogled us when we walked in? The one guy's jaw dropped, and the rise in his blood pressure caused his monocle to fog up."

"He's yours," Meeker announced.

"We'll see about that. Seriously, what are we going to do? I've been saving all my charms for someone who actually loves me."

"We'll cross that bridge when we come to it. Until someone knocks on that door and drags us out, we'll just stay here." As she ran a comb through her hair, she pushed the conversation in a new direction. "If you have a year and you worked as an officer in a bank, what's the easiest way to steal a thousand dollars?"

"What?" Bobbs' brow creased. "Helen, there are a dozen Nazis waiting down there to paw us, and you're asking a math question."

"I've been thinking about this on the plane ride over," Meeker explained. "I want you to think about it too. If you had all year to steal a thousand dollars and you worked at the bank, how would you do it?"

"I don't know. And to be honest, I don't care. I don't have enough clothing on to make a shawl, and you're thinking about robbing a bank. Have you lost it, or is this just your way of coping?"

"Wait, let me explain. If you wanted that thousand dollars and you had fifty-two weeks, you'd just take five dollars a day. That way you have the best chance of it not being noticed. In other words, you wouldn't take it all at once."

"Okay," the blonde replied, moving to her friend's side, "but what does that have to do with our situation right now? Is this your way of laying out a plan to escape and I'm missing the point? As your sister would say, 'Make with the music and hit me with the chorus.'"

"I'm not sure what that means, but I was just thinking about the missing gold at Fort Knox. The easiest way to steal it would be a few bars at a time, and then replace those bars with the ones that are just-gold plated each time you did it."

"Okay, it's easy to slip a five-dollar bill out of a bank, but how do you get heavy gold bars in and out of a secure government facility?"

"I haven't figured that out yet," Meeker admitted, "but there has to be something that comes into the base with supplies that could leave with the gold."

"And about the two missing men?" Bobbs argued. "If the operation was this smooth, what happened to them?"

"One of two things," Meeker suggested. "They were the masterminds, and when they got enough they just took off. Or rather than being bad guys, they were the ones who discovered what happened and were killed. If that's the case, they're likely buried somewhere on the base."

"Helen, let's hope we get back from our European vacation and have the chance

to test your theory. You'll forgive me if at this moment I don't care. After all, I'm dressed in what amounts to thin lingerie and surrounded by enough Nazis to stage a good-sized May Day parade."

Meeker smiled. "Just something to think about."

A knock on the door caused both women to jump. As Meeker's throat went dry and her heart rate rose, the left side of the double entry opened and a tall, thin S.S. officer, his face cold, eyes dark, and jaw set, studied the women and then barked out an order. Meeker understood just enough German to realize he was demanding they accompany him downstairs. Evidently the party was about to begin. Meeker stepped behind the man and in front of Bobbs. Eighteen long steps later she was at the entry to a smoke-filled drawing room crowded with Nazi officers. She'd never felt so uncomfortable.

As if putting the women on display, the officer had them stand at the base of the steps for at least a minute. The men whose eyes were now locked onto them began to point and whisper, yet none of them stepped forward. Then, with no warning, their escort grabbed Meeker and Bobbs by the arms and pushed them around the corner and down the hall.

What was next? Was the viewing just a preview? Was there going to be an auction to decide which of the men won the two women? As the team leader considered how best to face what she anticipated would be a humbling and degrading fate, she carefully eyed her surroundings, hoping to spot a possible escape route. The first door they passed was a billiards room. Standing well behind the table near the back wall was a

pair needing no introductions. The balding be-speckled man dressed in a regal Schutzstaffel uniform was Heinrich Himmler. Though he more resembled a milk-toast bookkeeper than a merciless tyrant, on most nights he would have been the most powerful man at any party. But just to his right, outfitted in a dark blue suit, was public enemy number one. Just seeing him caused Meeker's blood to run cold.

Unlike Himmler who was smiling, Adolf Hitler appeared as though he'd just swallowed something that didn't agree with him. The German leader, who'd been chatting with Himmler, looked up in time to catch Meeker's gaze. The awkward smile he aimed her way caused an immediate numbing chill. For the second time in a span of a few weeks, she felt as if she'd stared into the devil's eyes. With the officer pushing her, Meeker quickly passed out of view of the man who'd brought so much death to the world. Yet the unsettling feeling of having his eyes locked on her continued until their march stopped in front of a ten-foot high, four-foot wide walnut door. Wordlessly their escort twisted the knob and signaled for the woman to enter. As the door swung open, two older German Luftwaffe officers, standing beside a desk drinking what appeared to be brandy, gazed at the women. From their expressions it looked as though they'd just won the Irish sweepstakes.

As the door closed behind them, leaving the women alone with the two officers in what was likely a formal parlor or library, Bobbs glanced over at Meeker and whispered, "I've never been fond of blind dates."

"It could be worse," Meeker whispered back, "though I'm not sure how."

CHAPTER 13

Saturday May 9, 1942
11:05 PM
Thirty miles outside Berlin, Germany

Though she had no idea what the men were saying, their intentions were obvious. Within seconds of the women being deposited in the room, the larger of the two officers shoved Meeker over to a large desk and clumsily attempted to kiss her. She turned her face just in time for his lips to strike her cheek. Resting her left hand on the desktop, she used her knee to provide some breathing room. As he swept in for another attack, she noted a rolled out series of blueprints on the desk. With his lips closing fast, she had no time to study them. As his fingers latched onto her shoulders, Meeker opted to change tactics. Rather than fight off his advances, she would meet them head-on. Dipping her lips into his, she let them linger there, running her hands through his thin, sparse hair before gently pushing him back and smiling. Putting her index finger to his mouth, Meeker grinned, spun around on the desk, placed her heels to the thickly carpeted floor and hurried to the door. Grabbing the key, she locked the entry and made a big show of dropping the key down the front of her dress. As they watched her, both men grinned.

They were now sure this night was about to get much better, and that is exactly what Meeker wanted them to believe. Their faces glowed even brighter as the woman bent forward, pulling her dress up above her knees. Holding the hem with her left hand, she smiled and winked, then reached under the garment and retrieved her gun from where

she'd tied it to her leg. A second later when Bobbs displayed her weapon, the men's faces turned gray.

"Becca, there are blueprints on the desk. I'm betting they're the reason for this little celebration. Would you be a dear and grab them? And ask our dates what this is all about."

Bobbs rushed over, retrieved the plans, and when her pistol was positioned right in front of the men, demanded to know what was in the blueprints. Showing little or no resolve, the surprised and quaking officers gave her a series of short answers.

"My date said these are plans to an experimental rocket," Bobbs explained as she moved back across the room toward Meeker.

"What did *my* date tell you?" Meeker asked.

"All he said was, 'I know nothing, I know nothing.'" Bobbs

shrugged. "Now what do we do about these guys?"

"I'll hold your gun; you grab the curtain sash and tie them up. Gag them, too."

While her partner secured the officers, Meeker walked over to the French doors and looked outside. They were about fifty feet from where Reese stood by their car.

"Becca," she said as she studied the landscape, "we have a problem."

After securing the final gag, the blonde rushed over to the doors and glanced outside. She nodded. "Our car's blocked in."

"You still good at hotwiring?"

"It goes with working in crime labs," Bobbs assured her.

"Do you see that Mercedes at the end of the drive, pointed in the direction we need to go?"

"The staff car with the Nazi flags?"

"That's our ride. Take the plans, get over to that car, and get it going. I'll get Henry."

The women opened the door and slipped out. From a small porch Meeker watched Bobbs scamper across the grass. The team leader held her ground until the blonde arrived at the large, gray staff car. Satisfied her friend was safe, Meeker hurried to where Reese stood. He'd just turned her way when she stepped out from under a tree and into an open area illuminated by a porch light.

"Now that's a dress," he announced with a smile.

"I'll let you wear it sometime," she shot back. "Becca's hotwiring a car over there. We need to get going." As she turned she saw a short uniformed man open the front door and step out onto the porch. Sensing a need to provide a reason why she was not inside, she turned, grabbed Reese, and pulled his mouth to hers. He needed no encouragement to play along with the adlibbed plan. Twenty seconds later she eased back and asked, "Is he gone?"

"Who cares?" Reese replied and kissed her again.

"Okay," Meeker whispered as she pulled back a second time, "this is fun, and you are obviously well trained in this type of work. But we need to run over to that car Becca's hotwiring. Besides, we can make more time for this later."

"Is that a promise?" "We'll talk about it."

He grinned. "Can you actually run in that number without it falling off?"

"I hope we don't have to find out." She almost kissed Reese again, but sensing the clock ticking, she turned and quickly moved across the grounds to the now running Mercedes. Sliding into the front seat beside the driver, she shut the door.

As Reese jumped into the backseat, Bobbs let the clutch out and headed the huge vehicle toward the road. As she rolled down the gravel drive, she asked, "What about Maria?"

"My guess is she'll be fine," Reese assured her. "I think that woman can take care of herself."

"And what about The Snake?" Meeker chimed in. "Until things went upside down, we were scheduled to meet him."

"We got the plates," Reese said. "The mission isn't a wash."

"And as a bonus we got some weapon plans," Bobbs added

as she turned left onto the road and headed toward the place where the men had stopped them earlier in the night. "Hey, they're still there. Without Maria, how are we going to talk our way through this time?"

"Have your gun ready," Meeker suggested. "I don't think visiting is an option."

Offering no debate or an alternative plan, Bobbs pushed the pedal down and dropped the car into second. It was hitting twenty as it approached the checkpoint. When one of the soldiers stepped out and waved at the trio, Bobbs smiled and waved back but didn't slow down. By the time she blew by the German enlisted man, she had the Mercedes up to thirty and the soldier's smile turned to a look of confusion.

With their vehicle picking up speed, Reese glanced over his shoulder and announced, "Several of them are piling in the truck to follow us."

"I didn't figure they'd just let us go," Meeker cracked.

"This crate can outrun the truck," Bobbs assured them. "We'll be out of sight within two minutes."

As Bobbs rammed her foot to the floor, the Mercedes lunged forward. In a matter of seconds, it was up to seventy-five. The woman grinned. "I've got to get me one of these." The words had no more than come out of her mouth when the trio heard what sounded like a rifle shot. A second later the car pulled hard to the right. As Meeker and Reese anxiously looked on, the driver tried to wrestle the two-ton car back onto the road. It was no use. With the passenger wheels already in the grass and the left front tire flat, their course was set.

"Hang on!" Bobbs screamed.

A split-second after her warning, the staff car rolled down the ditch and slammed into a stone fence. The impact pushed the radiator into the engine and caused a half- dozen large pieces of rock to fly into the woods. Throwing her door open, Meeker staggered out, gun drawn, her eyes fixed on the fast-approaching truck that was now only about two hundred yards away. Reese was the next to crawl from the vehicle; Bobbs, her face bleeding from a gash on her forehead, followed.

"Custer at Little Big Horn or the Americans at the Alamo?" Meeker asked as she and the other two crouched behind the battered but still upright Mercedes.

Reese looked over his shoulder. "If we get into those woods, we'll have a better chance. Might even be able to work our way to the plane."

Meeker looked to Bobbs. "You got the weapon plans?"

"They're in the car. I'll get them."

"Wait!" Reese reached into his coat and jerked out the engraving plates. After handing them to Meeker, he announced, "You two can't move very fast in those dresses, so get over that fence and into the woods. I'll grab the plans."

Seeing no reason to argue with sound logic, Meeker shot a final look at the approaching truck, now less than one hundred feet from their position, turned, crawled over the fence, and dropped to the ground. She waited as Bobbs shinnied up the four-foot high barrier and awkwardly fell to the grass beside her. The women then hurriedly moved a dozen steps toward the woods. A second later the athletic Reese leapt up on the fence.

"Here are the plans," he announced, tossing them to Bobbs.

A split-second later a shot rang out. Reese froze, his face framed by a sense of panic before blood began rushing from his mouth. Two more shots followed, both catching the agent in the back. Like a boxer who'd just taken a knock-out blow, he teetered on the top of the stone wall for a moment and then fell backwards.

Meeker rushed toward the fence, but before she could make the leap to the top, Bobbs grabbed her. "He's dead," she shouted. "We can't help him now. We've got a mission to complete."

Meeker, her mind fogged in a combination of confusion and rage, stepped back.

Was there really nothing she could do?

"Come on, Helen!" Bobbs screamed as she fired a couple of rounds over the fence toward the approaching truck.

With tears clouding her eyes, Meeker turned from the fence and pushed into the woods. As the brush tore at her dress, she continued to move deeper into the trees.

Alongside her, gun drawn and ready for action, was Bobbs.

"Got to get back to the plane," the blonde said.

The pair continued stumbling through the woods until they arrived at a meadow.

Breathing hard they stood in the shadows and sized up their situation. The road was about a hundred feet to their left. On it two German staff cars were racing along, followed by four troop trucks.

"That must be Himmler and Hitler," Bobbs noted.

Meeker didn't care who was in the vehicles or where they were going. In fact at that moment she didn't care if she lived or died. She was numb, cold, and broken. Her will to fight and even to breath were gone. If her friend hadn't been by her side, she would have fallen to the ground and given up.

"Okay," Bobbs urged, "we still have time to hike back to the plane. Let's get moving."

As the caravan disappeared around a hill, a huge explosion lit up the night sky.

Turning in unison toward the estate, the women watched flames shoot a hundred feet into the air.

"The Snake just bit again," Bobbs announced. "Guess he was able to change his plans in time to do some damage."

"Yeah," Meeker answered. "But he wasn't in time to save Henry."

CHAPTER 14

Sunday, May 10, 1942
12:45 AM
Thirty miles outside Berlin, Germany

Meeker and Bobbs cautiously crossed the isolated meadow and approached the barn where they hoped their ride home was still waiting. Meeker's already broken spirit was completely crushed when she saw no signs of life. There was now no doubt her plan had turned into a complete disaster. If there had been a cliff nearby, she would have jumped off.

"The explosion might have caused him to leave early," Bobbs noted.

"Couldn't blame him," Meeker whispered. At this moment she didn't care what happened to her, but she couldn't give up until Bobbs was safe. Two deaths in one day were more than she could possibly handle. Taking a deep breath, as much to steel her resolve as to regain her focus, she looked around the scene before them. At least they still appeared to be alone. Pointing to the barn she suggested, "Let's take a look. If the plane is gone, we need to get moving too."

"Yeah," the blonde cracked. "Dressed like this we'll easily blend in with the locals. No one will look our way and think we're anything other than two poor peasant girls."

Trying to ignore Bobbs' attempts to lighten the mood and soothe her aching heart, Meeker cracked open one of the large swinging doors and peered inside. While she saw

and heard nothing, at least the hay they'd moved to hide the plane was still there. With her gun leading the way, she took two steps forward.

"Stay right there," a deep voice ordered. It wasn't their pilot.

"It's a trap, Becca," Meeker yelled. Crouching against the wall, she tried to assess the situation. Had the Germans anticipated where they would come? Did they discover the plane and kill the pilot? How many were there? In the pitch-black building she had no way of knowing. The only thing she was sure of was that once more she'd bitten off more than she could chew.

"Helen Meeker?" the voice called again. This time she could tell it was from someone near the back wall.

"Who wants to know?" Meeker demanded.

"You're fine," the man's voice assured them. "No one is going to hurt you. Just hold your fire, and I'll prove it."

She wanted to trust what was said, but she knew she couldn't. After all, she didn't know the voice, and while the man spoke English, his accent was heavy and Germanic.

With both grief and shock clouding her thoughts, she gripped her gun a bit tighter. If she died, so be it, but she was going to die fighting. She would not be taken alive. She was not going to give up or give in. And dying on the same night as Henry almost seemed poetic.

"Maria," the man shouted, "go calm down your friends."

Stepping from the shadows, still wearing her black party dress, the tall, blonde woman smiled. "Helen, the man who you came to meet is here. You and Miss Bobbs just

have to walk over to the side of the barn. As you talk to him, our men will help your pilot move the plane out into the field."

Lowering her Colt, her eyes now somewhat adjusted to the darkness, Meeker finally spied the figure of a short, blocky man dressed in dark clothing on the far side of the building. Walking slowly forward, she forced a grim smile. "Are you The Snake?"

"The Nazis call me that. And it would be best if that is all you knew me by as well."

"I guess you know why I'm here."

"You are Helen Meeker," he announced. "You want me to tell you more about the agent who helped us get the fuel formula."

"Yes."

"He was quiet. Yet he was also a man with great confidence and a sense of duty. Unlike most of those I work with, death did not scare him. Though I am not much of a religious man, I got the idea he sensed there was a life beyond this one. Maybe that is why he wore the strange leather bracelet on his right wrist. I guess that cross symbolized his faith. I remember noting it the first time we shook hands."

"And the Bible verse," Bobbs added as she joined them, "likely sealed your opinion as well."

"The Bible verse?"

"The one carved into the leather," Meeker explained.

"I wasn't aware of that," he admitted. "You know what else was funny. He wasn't wearing the band the night we shook hands for the final time. Even though he was

wearing a jacket, I know I would have seen it. I thought it was his good luck charm. Perhaps he took it off, and that is why he died."

"Did he take the microfilm back with him?" Bobbs asked.

"Yes. When Strickland contacted me and told me he had not found it, I checked the boat, but it was not there."

"And he couldn't have given it to anyone else?" Meeker asked.

The man leaned against the wall, crossed his thick arms, and shook his head. "No. I was the only one who accompanied him to England. Earlier in the week he put the film in a small metal capsule not any bigger than a child's marble. In fact, it might have been smaller. That night on our trip across the channel I asked him about it, and he assured me it was in the safest place in the world."

Bobbs looked toward Meeker. "Guess we're no farther along than we were back in the States. Wonder what happened to it."

Before Meeker could reply The Snake said, "I hate to see my most important mission result in nothing gained for the cause of freedom."

"Not a total loss," Meeker assured him. "The Germans don't have it either, so I guess the glass is half-full."

"Interesting way to look at it," he noted.

The three stood in the darkness, each seemingly lost in thought until they heard footsteps behind them. As if part of a drill team, the trio turned in unison toward the door.

"The plane's ready," Maria called out. "You need to get out of here before the Nazis finish fighting that fire."

"Thank you," Meeker said as she once more looked to the man. "I do appreciate your work."

"I understand you lost a team member tonight," he replied. "I am very familiar with that experience."

Her eyes misting, Meeker nodded.

"My men have his body," The Snake assured her. "We took out the German soldiers just as they were about to go over a stone wall and into the woods. I will guarantee your friend will be properly buried with all honors due a hero."

"Thank you," Meeker whispered. She took a deep breath and choked out, "He was a good man and an even better partner. I loved him."

CHAPTER 15

Sunday, May 10, 1942
8:35 PM
Columbia, Missouri

An impatient Alistar Fister studied Dr. Warren Williams. The professor had been working for two full days, transferring the information from the map drawn more than four centuries before by the Caddo Tribe to a current Rand McNally Arkansas roadmap. When would he finish? Or perhaps he really had no clue how to decipher it. A ringing phone pulled Alistar's gaze from Williams to the other side of the room.

"Could you get that?" the professor asked.

"Sure." Alistar ambled to a small table and picked up the receiver. "Hello."

"I'm looking for Mr. Riley O'Mally."

Alistar recognized Bauer's voice. "It's me, and to answer your unasked question, no, he has not found the spot yet. He's still working on it."

"How long is it going to take?"

"Hey, at least you're not the one holed up here waiting in a house with a dead Indian woman. I'll call you when we have something." Alistar didn't bother saying goodbye before placing the phone's receiver back into the cradle. Across the room Williams put his pencil down, rubbed his eyes, and looked at his guest.

"I believe I've found it." The man's voice showed the signs of a long weekend without sleep.

"Where is it?"

"It's north central Arkansas outside of Mountain View. The spring isn't on any of the relief or mineral surveys I've looked at, but based on the current roadmap, it shouldn't be that hard to find. My guess is that it's been hiding in plain sight."

Alistar walked over to the older man's desk. He studied the map and nodded. "We can easily get there tomorrow."

"That part is doable," Williams agreed. "But the thing standing in our way is that this location appears to be on private property. I doubt the owners would take too kindly to our knocking on their door and asking to explore their farm. And most likely these folks aren't dumb either. If they think there's something valuable on their place, they'll want a piece of the action."

"There are ways around that, Professor. Just like there were ways to spirit that Indian woman away from the mountain. Now may I?" Alistar asked while pointing to the map. "I'd like to compare it to the original. You know, just for educational purposes."

Williams leaned back in his chair and nodded. "Feel free. Tomorrow we can drive down, find out who owns the property, and hopefully get them to let us look around. If we find the spring, we can bring some water back here for analysis."

As Alistar picked up the two maps, he glanced over at a table in the far corner of the cluttered room. Resting on the six-foot oak library desk was the body of the Caddo woman. Though it made no sense, after she'd been dead for decades, he couldn't wait to get away from her. She was so well-preserved it looked as though she could open her eyes, rise, and talk.

"Professor, what are you going to do with her?"

"The map might have been your objective," Williams said, his eyes falling onto Kawutz, "but she's far more interesting to me. I'll spend months getting to know her, examining every facet of her body and clothing, doing every test I know to help me determine her story." He paused, wiped his eyes, and smiled. "When you've spent as long as I have looking for her, you want to relish every moment. I've dreamed of having her in my grasp for decades, and now—" The buzz of the door-bell caused the man's attention to move from the dead woman to the entry hall. "I wonder who that could be."

"I'll step into the kitchen," Alistar suggested. "And I think you might want to keep them from seeing her body."

Williams got up, grabbed a large blanket, and covered Kawutz. As he walked wearily toward the front door, Alistar took the maps and stepped out of the room.

Standing with the kitchen door slightly ajar, he watched his host open the home's front door. Filling the entry was a powerfully built dark-skinned man, at least six and a half feet tall and likely weighing two hundred and fifty pounds. Just behind the giant was a small older woman, her eyes dark, her skin reddish, and her back ramrod straight.

"Sue," the professor announced, "I didn't expect you, but I do have news."

The visitors didn't wait for an invitation to enter. With no warning and little effort, the man shoved the professor to the side and marched into the hall. Pausing, he studied the entries into four different rooms before seeing the light coming from the office.

"You can't go in there," Williams shouted.

"Dr. Williams," the woman declared, "you can't stop him from doing whatever he wants."

The professor ignored the warning and grabbed the large man's arm. The giant shook off the professor's grip as if he were nothing more than a toddler. After bouncing off a wall, Williams watched helpless, his mouth agape, as the huge visitor entered the lit room, stopped as if getting his bearings, then walked directly to the table. Tossing back the blanket revealed the body of the Caddo woman.

Sue, her expression placid and calm, stepped around the professor and entered the office. She studied Kawutz, shook her head, and then turned back to Williams.

"You swore you wanted nothing more than to honor my tribe's history."

He nodded. "The information that will come from my work will do just that." The woman spat at the professor's feet. "You took her from sacred ground." "It was necessary to learn what must be learned," Williams explained.

Sue's eyes were aflame. Pointing toward the professor, she said, "My grandmother used to live by this code. A burial is a sacred thing. Once a body has entered the ground, it is to stay there. If it is removed, then another must replace it. You have removed a body; therefore, yours will replace it."

As Alistair watch through the cracked door, the woman signaled her companion with a slight wave of her right hand. Moving with the speed and grace of a cat, the giant grabbed Williams by the throat and slowly pulled him off his feet. He let his captive dangle there, his toes just off the ground, as he closed his hands more tightly around the smaller man's neck. Silently the woman watched the life slowly drain from the professor's body. When Williams went completely limp, his attacker dropped him to the floor.

Alistar saw no reason to step out from his hiding place. He had what he wanted, and that meant he had no further use for the professor. Having someone else close the man's mouth meant he didn't need to get his own hands dirty. Now all he needed was to find out what the visitors would do next.

"Take Kawutz's body," Sue ordered as she looked around the room. "Once we get her out of the house, we'll burn it to the ground."

"Why did you lead him to her?" the man asked as he scooped up Kawutz in his

arms.

"I wanted to see what he knew. I wanted to test his character. I had to know if he really cared about our history and our people, or if he was just another white man who had no respect for our ways. Finding her resting place is one thing, but stealing her body and removing her spirit from that mountain is another." She shrugged. "A body for a body, and a life for a life."

Her large companion nodded. "I understand."

"Take him, too," Sue announced as she turned and walked from the room. "He will not rest in sacred ground; he will be left for the vultures. After all, he is as they are— something that lives by picking the meat off the dead."

Sensing he knew all he needed to know, Alistar silently crept out the back door.

After slinking across the yard, he slid into the professor's station wagon, started the Packard's whisper-quiet motor, and pulled into the alley behind the house. He was a block away before he switched on the lights.

CHAPTER 6

Monday, May 11, 1942
11:00 AM
London, England

In a small bedroom off the kitchen of a modest home on the west side of London, Helen Meeker managed a few hours of fitful sleep only to be awakened by gunfire echoing through her dreams. She then sat alone at a small dining table, sipping lukewarm tea and listening to music from a console radio. The latest tune to fill the nine-inch speaker was the classic Ink Spots' hit "We Three, My Echo, My Shadow, and Me." This song about loneliness hit her like a ton of bricks. There had been three that left together on the mission, but only two came back.

"I see you're awake," Russell Strickland announced as he strolled through the backdoor of the cottage he'd occupied since being transferred from Washington in December.

She nodded. "Not sure I'll ever sleep well again."

Her host pulled back a chair and joined the woman at the table. He drummed his fingers on the wood until the song ended. Once the final word had been sung, he noted, "Mr. Reese seemed like a good man. I figure that's what you're thinking about. After all, it's only in moments of sadness or pain that a brow wrinkles like yours is now."

"He was more than a good man," Meeker whispered. "He was my partner."

"And he did what partners do," Strickland added. "He gave his life for you. If the situation were reversed, you'd have done the same for him."

"Yeah, that's true." She sighed. "If that's supposed to make me feel better, you might want to trot out a new trite line. And I don't want to hear any of the stuff about how he knew the dangers, that he signed up for them. The fact is, I demanded this mission, I fought for it, and Henry wasn't a part of my plans. He only came along for the ride because the president made me bring him. The president didn't believe two women could take care of that job on their own and we needed a man. I guessed I proved him right too."

"I understand," the tall middle-aged agent answered. "And the president felt horrible when he found out. I know that for a fact because I made the call to the White House and told him."

Meeker looked up from the teacup into the man's blue eyes. "And what did we gain? I used retrieving the engraved plates as a ticket to get me on this adventure, but you could have gotten them back another way. And The Snake offered us nothing on the formula. He doesn't have it. So Henry died for nothing."

"Not true," the OSS agent argued while still keeping his tone even. "The plans for the new rocket you found might be experimental in nature, but they show us the direction the Nazis are heading. Who knows how many lives will be saved with our being able to study those plans and adapt them for our use."

He got up, crossed the room, and switched off the radio. As he walked back to the table, Strickland continued his seemingly motivational speech. "And Miss Meeker, something else you might find interesting is that the car you stole in your getaway was a ctually Hitler's. After The Snake's team ambushed the Germans who killed your friend, they discovered some war plans in the wreck that uncovered unknown gun emplacements along the French coastline. So all things considered you did a whale of a job. In fact you did more in a few hours than my teams usually do in months."

"But," she argued, "we didn't get what we went after. I'm no closer to finding the formula than I was before we left." She studied her host for a second before adding, "And perhaps the Germans are on the verge of getting it back."

"Maybe you should blame me for that," Strickland suggested. "After all I failed to get to the coast in time to save Clark's life. I was held up five minutes due to a flat tire, and because of that a man lost his life and the Allies didn't get control of the formula.

How do you think that makes me feel?"

She nodded again. "The formula has cost both of us good friends."

"Yeah. And it will likely cost a lot more lives too. That's war. That's the horrible price of men feeling that the spilling of human blood is worth claiming land in the name of either God or country."

"Russell, were you with Clark when he died? I mean, did you talk to him at all?

Did he say anything?"

"Not much," Strickland explained with a mournful shrug. "He was all but gone when I got there. He did manage to joke a bit though. That was his nature. He liked to leave each of our meetings by, as the Brits say, 'cracking wise.' And this time it wasn't funny."

"What was his last joke?"

"He told me to make sure and check his pulse." Choking on his words the OSS agent continued. "He knew he was nearly dead, and he asked me to check his stupid pulse. As I remember it he even pushed his left hand toward me a bit. And then he quoted Shakespeare."

"Really?"

"Yeah. He said, 'Goodnight sweet prince.'"

Her blue eyes locked onto his. "Did that mean anything to you? Could it have been a code?"

Strickland shook his head. "I've thought about that a lot. There was a Prince Albert tobacco tin in his pocket, and I went over it about a half-dozen times. Had the lab look at it too. But there was nothing."

"That was a line from *Hamlet*, wasn't it?"

"Yeah. 'Now cracks a noble heart. Good-night, sweet prince; and flights of angels sing thee to thy rest.'"

Meeker contemplated the line as she took another sip of tea. What was so special about *Hamlet* that a dying American had repeated a line from that ancient play as the life faded from his body? She looked back to her host. "What about the play? Was there anything in it that might offer us a hint as to where he might have hidden the microfilm?"

"Helen," the OSS agent explained, "since that horrible night I've read that play so many times I could take to the stage and fill any of the roles. I've analyzed each line and carefully looked at the piece as if it were code. I've brought our experts in too. No one has come up with anything."

Meeker frowned. "By the way, did you check his pulse?"

"No," Strickland admitted. "I even let him down when it came to his last wish." He paused and licked his lips before asking, "What were Henry's last words?"

"Here are the plans," she replied. "There was no symbolism there. He was just tossing me the blueprints we'd found at the party."

The room went silent as the two people sitting at the table considered the "what ifs" that would never be. With each minute becoming another and another, Meeker slipped deeper into a fog of regrets. Holding her head in her hands, she fought back screams of agony and tears of loss. She now hated the mission she had begged for, the war that had stripped her of a normal life, the fact she'd let so many people down, and even the manner in which she flung away a sensible woman's world to try to become something more. The president once told her that every day he thought about all the good men and women he'd sent into war and how many of them would never live to see victory. He mourned with all the widows and children, as well as mothers and fathers left behind due to his decisions. Their faces and screams even haunted him when he slept.

And now she knew exactly what he meant. Even if Henry Reese died for his country, he was still just as dead, and what comfort was there in that?

"What's the answer?" she whispered. "You mean, to where the formula is?"

"No," Meeker moaned. "What's the answer we need to find so we can end all this madness? How many graves have to be dug and prayers have to be said to convince people that wars don't solve problems? All they do is bring pain and suffering."

"I don't know," he admitted. "I saw him, you know." "Saw who?"

Meeker lifted her face and looked into the agent's. "Hitler. He was there, and I saw him. Our eyes met; I felt his gaze on mine. Why didn't I just have the courage to pull out my gun and shoot him?"

"You would have died," Strickland said.

"But think how many others might have lived. I had the chance, and I failed humanity."

"Maybe," the man noted, "your living means even more to the world's future than Hitler's dying." He paused, rose from his chair, put his hand on Meeker's shoulder, and said, "You need to get Miss Bobbs up and get ready. I'll be taking you to the airfield for the flight home in less than an hour."

Home. The word pierced her heart. What would home be like without Henry

Reese?

CHAPTER 17

Monday, May 11, 1942
1:15 PM
Mountain View, Arkansas

On Sunday night Alistar Fister drove the Packard station wagon to Batesville, Arkansas, rented a room at a local hotel, got a good night's sleep, and was at the courthouse the moment the doors opened the next morning. Paying little attention to the beautiful spring weather, he studied several different property maps before identifying the owner of the parcel he needed to explore. A quick lunch at a local café gave him the fuel needed to begin what he hoped would lead him to an elusive fountain that men had searched for since the beginning of time. Yet a twenty-mile drive down a series of red clay roads only took Fister to an undeveloped patch of ground filled with acres and acres of rolling hills and post oak trees. Unlike the other places he'd passed along the way, this one was protected by a tall wire fence. Worse yet a large imposing metal gate blocked the entrance to a narrow dirt lane.

Stopping the Packard opposite the property, Alistar stepped into the afternoon sunlight and studied the scene. Every twenty feet someone had nailed large "No Trespassing" signs. At the bottom of each of the wooden markers were the additional words, "Violators Will Be Shot Without Warning." So much for the welcome wagon!

The sound of a motor shifted the visitor's attention from the gate to the road.

Chugging up a long hill to his right was a decade-old Ford truck hauling a load of logs.

As it neared the driver slowed the vehicle, shut off the engine, and jumped from the cab. The tall lean man, dressed in jeans and a blue work shirt, smiled as he crossed the road.

"You having car trouble?"

"No," Alistar assured him. "I was just wondering about this piece of property. I was hoping to visit with the owners."

The man smiled. "I'm Hank Evans, and I've lived in this part of the world for more than fifty years. Been coming by this piece of land for nigh that long as well. I can tell you for sure that nobody gets on this place and lives to tell about it."

Alistar frowned. "Can't see why. I mean, it doesn't look like it's worth much."

The friendly stranger shrugged. "Most of us don't think it's worth the cost of the fencing. Soil is poor, can't grow anything worth eating or selling, but the folks who own this place guard it like it's the Bank of England."

Fister nodded. "Mr. Evans, do they have a home back there behind those trees?" "There's a hired man who lives there, and he has a pack of dogs that'll either tree or tear up any person who dares cross that fence, but the owners rarely come up here. They live in New Orleans and have had this property for more than a century. In fact Anthony Corelle bought this land from the French before the U.S. even had control of it."

When a pack of hounds began baying in the distance, both men turned their heads to the south. The dogs sounded vicious.

"The hounds of hell," Evans announced. "That's what those dogs are. They're as mean as the caretaker. And there are so many of them, even if you had a machinegun, you'd run out of bullets before you got 'em all."

"So," Alistar said as he leaned back against the Packard, "why is the land so important to the Corelle family? What are they hoarding in there?"

"You'd have to ask them," the man answered. "Maybe it's because they've owned it since before white men even thought about moving here, but I kind of think it's something else. A truck comes up every few weeks, picks something up, and leaves. The bed's covered, so we don't know what it is, but it's been happening all my life. My grandfather watched horse-drawn wagons do the same thing when he was a child." He shook his head. "And nobody ever saw that cargo and lived to tell about it."

"The Corelle Family." Alistar tried again to peer through the thick woods. "I take it they have money."

"I don't know what they've got," Evans answered. "The folks that have been to New Orleans say people down there talk of Anthony Corelle in whispers. It's almost like they're afraid to even say his name out loud." The man smiled and nodded, turned, and walked back toward his truck. When he opened the door and stepped onto the running board, he looked back at Alistar. "Your accent tells me you're not from around here, so that means you might think all I've said is just another ignorant hillbilly legend. But let me assure you of this. If you go back in those woods, a fisherman will find your body in the White River—if anybody finds it at all. So if you want to explore that property, you better have the whole U.S. Marine Corp with you."

Alistar nodded and waved as Evans drove off. After the truck was out of site and the dust had once more settled on the road, he turned his attention back to the gate. For the moment maybe just locating where the map led was enough. He'd put off drinking from the well for a while and let Bauer chart the next move.

CHAPTER 18

Tuesday, May 12, 1942
12:50 PM
Outside Drury, Maryland

Her hair uncombed, wearing no make-up, dressed in light pink pajamas and a long terrycloth white robe, Helen Meeker sat, all balled up, on the corner of the couch, her dark blue eyes locked on the radio's dial. Though she'd seen him shot, watched his blood shoot from his body, and witnessed him tumble off the fence and into enemy hands, she simply couldn't fully grasp the fact that Henry Reese was dead. She half expected him to waltz in now, a crooked grin on his face, proclaiming he'd fought off six Germans and escaped. If The Snake hadn't told her his men had seen the body, Meeker might somehow have believed that fantasy. But somewhere behind enemy lines in Germany, likely in an almost forgotten meadow or deep in the woods, the FBI agent was resting under the dirt, and it was all her fault. If only she hadn't pushed to go on that crazy mission.

Ever since they'd returned she'd been numb. She also had no desire to sleep or eat. The strains of music jumping from the Zenith's speaker bounced off her rather than resonate in her mind or soul. She recognized she'd lost her will to live, yet for reasons she couldn't understand, her lungs and heart kept working.

"Hey, kid." Becca Bobbs spoke softly as she entered the room. "How you feeling?"

Meeker didn't look at her friend as she wrapped her arms around her knees and pulled them close to her chest. Finally, as the silence grew awkward, she muttered, "I don't really feel anymore."

"Yeah," Bobbs replied as Meeker looked her way. "I can understand that. Just thought you'd like to know Churchill is doing handstands over getting the engraving plates back, and our Air Force took out those gun emplacements in a bombing raid last night. I understand we'd be getting medals for our work if anyone actually knew we were alive." She paused, bit her lip, and turned away from her friend. "I'm sorry; I didn't mean to go there."

Meeker shrugged. "Why avoid it? Henry's dead. I know that. You and I saw it happen. And no matter how many lives we saved by finding those plans or getting those plates back, it doesn't make me feel any better."

"Yeah, I know." Bobbs smoothed her gray sailor dress and sat down beside Helen. "But you're still the team leader; we still need you to make decisions. As much as I'd like to let you spend a long time allowing your mental wounds to heal, I can't do that. This is war, and we have a job to do."

"I don't want to lead anymore," Meeker mumbled. "I don't want anyone to take chances because of my hunches or whims. I don't want to give orders and have people die."

"Helen," Bobbs said as she placed her hand on Meeker's shoulder, "you have to.

That's just the way it goes. The president believes in you, and so do I. Even as you sit here, there are decisions to make. I just came up from the lab, and Dr. Ryan wants to know if he can send Shelton Clark's body back to Magnolia. In other words, are we finished with it? Is it time to let the agent rest in peace? I can't make that call. I don't have the authority, but you do."

"Yeah," she announced, resting her chin on her knees. "The body didn't give us anything anyway. We're still no closer to getting the formula."

Bobbs nodded. "Spencer also wants to know if you'd like the leather band he cut off Clark's left wrist. When I told the doctor the story of The Snake, he thought you might want to find a way to get it back to him. The Snake might want to wear that bracelet as a way of honoring Clark."

Meeker pushed her tousled hair from her face. Staring at the floor, her tone emotionless, she said, "Yeah, let's send it back to Strickland and have him find a way to get it behind enemy lines. It might serve as an inspiration to have the strange band that Clark wore on his—" She stopped, her mouth agape and her eyes wide open. The fog that had dulled her mind for the past few days was suddenly gone. Nearly leaping from the couch, she raced out the door, down the hall, and ran barefoot over the steps leading to the basement.

"Spencer," Meeker called out as she moved quickly across the room to the doctor's corner of the lab. "I need something clarified."

The man looked up from where he sat at his desk, his face mirroring shock and confusion. He was evidently still searching for something to say when the guest fired off a quick verbal volley.

"You said you cut the leather band off Clark's left wrist. Are you sure it wasn't his right?"

"No," he assured her. Getting up he moved to a file cabinet, opened a drawer, and pulled a folder. He thumbed through his notes before pointing to something he'd jotted down during his examination. "It was on his left wrist. I have photos I took when the body first arrived that Becca can develop if you need to see it."

"I'm sure," Meeker replied, "you know the facts. It's just that The Snake told us Clark always wore it on his right wrist. Yet he also remembered that night on the boat when they crossed the Channel that it wasn't on his right arm. Why did he change it to his left?"

"I don't know—unless it was to cover up an injury. Maybe he used it to help stop the bleeding of a cut I noted under that band."

"Okay," Meeker said, her hand going to her chin. "That does

make sense. Let me think for a moment. Strickland said Clark's last words were from Hamlet, but before that he asked Strickland to check his pulse." She snapped her fingers. "You check a pulse either at the neck or the wrist. Where's the leather band?"

The doctor moved quickly to his desk, opened a cigar box, and pulled out the bracelet. Before he could turn around, the woman was at his side and jerked it out of his hands.

She studied the verse crudely carved into the band and grimaced. "The Snake remembered the cross but not the scripture. Look at this," she announced as she held it up to the doctor's eyes. "This isn't just crudely cut into the leather; it's also fairly recent.

The exposed leather hasn't aged yet."

Walking over to the empty surgery table, she set the bracelet down and ran her fingers over it. There were no telltale bumps, no newly cut slots or secret places to hide microfilm. As she turned the item over to recheck for hiding places, Bobbs walked down the stairs and joined them.

"Becca," Meeker said, "what are the words to Hebrews 1:11? I know you recited them last week, but I've forgotten them."

The blonde moved closer, looked down at the leather band, and recited. "'Now faith is the substance of things hoped for, the evidence of things not seen.'"

"Not seen . . ." Meeker considered those words. "He moved the band to the left wrist for a reason. The microfilm is not in the leather, so where could it be?"

"I think I know," Ryan whispered just loud enough to be

heard.

As the women watched, the man grabbed his surgical scissors and walked over to a small walk-in freezer. The doctor opened the door and stepped in beside a gurney where the agent's body rested. Pulling back a white sheet, exposing the agent from the waist up, the doctor grabbed Clark's left arm. He studied the stitches on the wrist before placing his thumb onto the spot of the wound. He pushed, nodded his head, and looked back to Meeker.

"There's something hidden here."

Grabbing the side of the gurney, Ryan pushed it out into the lab. After closing the freezer door, he looked at the woman. "Come over and look at this." With Meeker on his right and Bobbs on his left, the doctor extended Clark's left arm. "There are five total wounds here. The four on the upper arm are ragged and were likely the result of some type of hand-to-hand combat, but this one on his wrist is smooth and clean, almost like a surgical cut."

While the women watched, Ryan sliced through the stitches, and the wound opened. He reached in and pulled out a small, shiny metal ball. After setting it on the gurney beside the body, he looked over at Meeker as if asking her to fill in the rest of the story.

"We now know," she announced, "why he asked Strickland to check his pulse." Glancing toward Bobbs, her tone now assertive, Meeker continued. "Figure out how to get that thing open, and make sure the film is there. If it is let's send it to the

White House. They can get it to the FBI, and our people can see if the formula works."

Bobbs picked up the small metal object. As she studied it, the team leader turned and headed toward the stairs. Just before she disappeared, the blonde called out, "Helen, don't you want to be with me as I open it?"

Meeker waved. "No, I need a bath and some food." She looked to the doctor. "Spencer, get cleaned up. I'm going to call Dr. Mills and arrange for Grace Lupino to have a visitor. I want you to spend a few days with her. Don't press the woman; she's in a fragile state. But keep digging until you come up with something we don't know about the man who's behind this. We have to figure out who he is and who he works for."

Meeker glanced from Ryan to Bobbs. "Where are Reggie and Clay?" "They're in New Orleans."

"Why?"

"Killpatrick, the FBI agent Henry used to work with, got a tip that a mysterious underworld figure in the city might be doing some dirty work for the Nazis," Bobbs explained. "Seems this guy has his hand on every facet of the crime world, but no one can pin anything on him."

"But why send our guys?"

Ryan jumped into the conversation. "Clay told me FDR wanted to see if this guy would react when he saw Reggie."

Meeker smiled. "If he does then that crime boss might also help us identify the power behind Alistar and Lupino." She turned to Bobbs. "We need to go to New Orleans too. I'll call

Dr. Mills and have him figure a way to get us there without being spotted."

A suddenly energized Meeker rushed up four steps before stopping and turning back to her team members. "When did they leave?"

"The day you went to England," Ryan explained. "They got the call about an hour after you left."

"Okay." Running her right hand through her hair, she looked back at the doctor. "And what is the crime boss's name?"

"Anthony Corelle."

"Becca," Meeker instructed, "touch base with Clay. Tell him we're coming down there."

Meeker didn't wait for an answer as she raced to her room. She couldn't bring Henry back—that was beyond her power— but if she was right and they had the formula, at least he'd died for their objective. That gave her a bit of comfort. Now it was time to move forward.

CHAPTER 19

Thursday, May 14, 1942
Noon
New Orleans, Louisiana

On a hot, humid day, Fredrick Bauer and Alistar Fister stood in the shade of the French Landing Hotel porch. As a few folks strolled down the sidewalks, and trucks carrying fish and produce chugged by on the downtown streets, the two spoke in hushed tones with a well-dressed, short, muscular, ebony-skinned man in his fifties. This was not a chance meeting. Micah Hopkins was more than just the best jazz trumpeter in the city; he was also the region's unofficial keeper of legend and lore. Though Bauer had been assured the local resident would, for the right price, be outgoing and helpful, at this moment the native Louisianan was eyeing him suspiciously.

"So," Hopkins said, "the hotel clerk tells me you boys want to know about a local family. We got a lot of powerful folks here on the river and down in the bayou, and I know them all as well as I know my own kinfolk. But in order for our conversation to move along with the speed of a northbound freight, you'll have to be a bit more specific."

"We can be specific," Bauer assured him. "Just wanted to make sure you were the man with the answers."

"My first observation," Hopkins noted, "is you should have worn something other than a black wool suit. This is a shirt-sleeves and cotton town. So for my first answer, I'd recommend you get a new wardrobe. I can suggest a few places. My cousin has a shop down in the Ninth Ward you might like."

"I'll try to remember that next time I come for a visit," Bauer said. "For the moment, the length of my stay and my need for additional clothes will depend upon what you can tell me. Now, Mr. Hopkins—"

"Call me Notes," the trumpeter interrupted. "Everyone does 'cause I can play the blues like nobody else. The notes I hit bring joy in times of pain. They speak to the soul. They can make you cry and laugh at the same moment. Everyone in this city knows Notes, and they all talk about my music."

"Okay, Notes," Bauer said before the man could continue his seemingly well- practiced speech. "I'll get right to the point. What do you know about the Corelle family?"

The trumpeter shook his head. "You best ask me about somebody else—anybody else. Nobody talks about them, and nobody should. The lucky ones who chat about that clan get their tongues cut out, and the rest pay with their lives. I need my tongue and my breath, if you follow what I mean."

"What's your price?" Bauer asked.

Hopkins shook his head. "Money has no value to a dead man. There are no banks in heaven."

"How about a thousand dollars?"

The short man rubbed his mouth, looked over his shoulder, and frowned. "I'd love to have the cash, I sure would, but I like breathing too. In fact I like breathing a whole lot more than I like money. I like breathing more than I like anything, including jazz and crawfish."

"Two thousand."

Hopkins leaned closer. "Let me get this straight. It takes a lot of money for me to tempt the devil."

"Five thousand."

The trumpeter frowned. "Maybe you're the devil. I mean, no one else ever tempted me like this." He glanced over his shoulder before whispering, "Let's see the cash." After Bauer counted out fifty C-notes and stuffed them into the trumpeter's hand, Hopkins whispered again. "There's a storage room at the back of the hotel. You follow me there."

With their guide leading the way, the two visitors walked around a corner, down a brick-covered alley, and through a wooden door. Only when they were inside the small dark room filled with cleaning supplies and with the door closed did Hopkins speak in hushed tones.

"You can't tell anyone I talked to you. I've got to have that promise, or you can have your money back."

"We won't say anything," Bauer agreed. "I'll never contact you again. I just want the information."

"Okay," Hopkins replied, "but I have to know why you want the dope on the Corelles."

Bauer looked to Alistar before spilling the reason for their trip. "They own some land in Arkansas we're interested in."

Hopkins shook his head. "You don't want to mess with this family, and you don't want to try to buy anything they have. They don't just possess land; they also possess souls. They're into voodoo and about every other evil thing ever invented. People pay the old man to bless them, and they also give him money for protection. If you don't then your property burns, you die, or maybe both. They own the local law, have them in their hip pockets. In fact everyone bows to the Corelles."

"So," Bauer noted, "I take it the family has considerable wealth."

"More than King Solomon. But it isn't just that. They're pure evil. Hitler would quake in his boots if he met Anthony Corelle face to face."

Bauer leaned closer until his nose was just inches from the trumpeter. "Tell me about the old man."

Hopkins opened the door and glanced down the alley. Seemingly satisfied that no one had followed them, he shut the door and spoke in whispers.

"He lives on the outskirts of town, in a home the family built in the 1840s. No one sees him much unless they're called in for a visit. When the family wants to conduct business off the property, a member of one of the younger generations does that. The only time the old man appears in public is when he comes to town in a horse-drawn coach at Mardi Gras. He goes to the Regal Hotel, sits alone on the balcony, and looks down at the parade. Sometimes he tosses out money, but he never says a word. He's always dressed in a dark, old-fashioned suit, high boots, and a floppy hat."

Bauer looked at Alistar. "Doesn't sound like an easy person to deal with."

"You hit the right note there," Hopkins chimed in. "And he doesn't sell anything; he just collects stuff. Some say he even buys and owns people. Folks are scared of him. And why shouldn't they be? He's been the most mysterious and powerful man in New Orleans for a long, long time."

"How old is he?" Bauer asked.

"No one knows that. They weren't keeping birth records back then. But I've met his great, great grandsons, so that should tell you something."

Bauer smiled. "He must be close to a hundred."

"He's a lot older than that," Hopkins assured him. "And he never changes. I've been within twenty feet of him at Marti Gras. He looks the same now as he did in the 1840s. I've seen a painting of him from back then too. I swear to you, Anthony Corelle doesn't age and he doesn't die. And if you're smart you'll get out of town without trying to meet him. Now I've told you all I know."

Hopkins turned toward the door, peaked out into the alley,

and scurried away. He never once looked back.

Bauer grinned. "It's amazing what people believe."

"What if it's true?" Alistar asked. "What if the old Indian woman and Corelle drank from the same well? What if the water really does have that kind of power?"

"It can't. But the story of Anthony Corelle is one that a certain German leader will buy hook, line, and sinker." He paused and looked into Alistar's eyes. "Tomorrow morning we'll take a look at the home of Mr. Corelle, but tonight we'll relax, enjoy good food, and listen to music."

After the tall man opened the door, the two exited the small storeroom and made their way back to the street. As he turned the corner and stepped up to the sidewalk, Bauer accidently rubbed shoulders with a man dressed casually in a light green shirt and white slacks.

"I beg your pardon," the stranger said as he stepped to the side.

Bauer nodded and kept moving. As they approached the entrance to their hotel, Alistar pulled his boss to the side and whispered, "I think that was Clay Barnes."

Turning on his heels, Bauer looked back to the corner. The stranger was no longer in sight.

CHAPTER 20

Friday, May 15, 1942
9:15 AM
New Orleans, Louisiana

Thanks to the president, Helen Meeker and Becca Bobbs were taken to Louisiana on a private train. During the day-and-a-half trip, the women shared stories of Henry Reese, caught up on their sleep, and discussed more theories concerning the mystery at Fort Knox. When they arrived in New Orleans, Reggie Fister, driving a tan 1939 Ford, picked them up. On the trek across town to the Royale Hotel, Reggie brought the women up to speed on what he and Clay Barnes had discovered during their week in the city.

"So," Meeker said, as she studied the unique flavor found on the streets of New Orleans, "you really spotted your brother down here?"

"Actually," Reggie corrected her, "I didn't. Clay saw him in the company of a tall, lean man, about fifty."

"Any idea who the other man was?" Meeker probed.

"None," the driver answered as he motored the V-8 sedan around a sharp corner. "No one in town even knows his name, so I'm guessing he's not local."

Meeker looked out the window at two tall women, likely in their fifties, wearing colorful dresses and large hats, and pushing carts. They were evidently street vendors selling cooked seafood.

"What about the thin man?" she asked as she continued to study the smiling women. "Does Clay think it could be the puppet master?"

"And," Bobbs cut in before Helen could get her answer, "speaking of Clay, where is he?"

"He's following my brother. When we arrive at the hotel, I expect we'll find a message from him telling us where to meet him."

A sudden humid breeze pushing through the car's open windows caught Meeker's auburn locks, causing them to cover her face. After pulling her hair back, she glanced over at Reggie and posed the question of the moment.

"What do you know about Corelle?"

"We know everything—and we know nothing. He runs this town, and he has his hands in everything — both legitimate and criminal. He must be smart because no one can connect him to anything. This is a town where there's still a lot of superstition, and he uses that to his advantage. Many people actually believe he's the voodoo king, that he has hundreds of dolls in his home, and through them controls the lives and deaths of scores of people."

"Spooky," Bobbs noted from the backseat.

Reggie smiled. "His hold is so great and his legend so large that he's blamed for almost every death and illness in town. He causes more nightmares than the boogie man."

"What about his connections to the Nazis?" Meeker asked.

"Nothing direct," the driver replied as they pulled up in front of their small Creole-style hotel. He waited for a horse-drawn fruit cart to pass before continuing. "In truth I don't think he'd work with the Nazis directly. But if they needed something smuggled out of the country, his organization would likely do it for the right money. The bottom line? The Corelles have no loyalty to any government. The old man is a power king who doesn't see things in a political sense; he shades everything in its benefit to his family."

"Reggie," Meeker noted, "you fibbed. You know a lot about him."

"Not really." He turned in his seat until their eyes met. "We know a great deal about his operation, but we know very little about the man." Reggie pulled a folder off the seat, opened it, and yanked out a picture. After studying the black-and-white image, he handed it to Meeker. "That is one of the photos we have of Anthony Corelle. It was taken during a Mardi Gras celebration, and that happens to be the only time each year he ever leaves his estate."

Meeker looked at the picture and handed it to Bobbs. Reggie

then picked up another photo and pushed it her way. "Here's a second shot of the old guy."

The team leader studied it for a second before passing it on. As Bobbs was looking it over, Meeker noted, "Not much difference in the two shots. And with the huge hat, it's hard to see any details."

"True," Reggie said. "And I have ten more that look pretty much the same. But there is a bit of difference you missed in those two shots."

"What's that?" Meeker asked.

"They were taken forty years apart."

"That's impossible!" Bobbs exclaimed. "He looks the same age in both photographs."

"He looks pretty much the same in all the photos we have," Reggie assured her. As he let the shock settle in, he pulled a final picture from the file. "Ladies, here's a print of a painting of Anthony Corelle, commissioned in 1839. He looked the same then too."

"What are you trying to say?" Meeker demanded.

"I'm not suggesting anything. I just want you to know that many of the locals believe Corelle never dies." He let that sobering thought hang in the air before asking, "Now would you like me to take you to your rooms?"

Meeker looked back at Bobbs and shook her head. "What's this all about? No man lives forever. Is this some darkroom trick?"

The blonde raised her eyebrows. "You're asking a woman

who's legally dead a question like that? I'm sensing some irony here."

"Mr. O'Toole!" a voice called out. Meeker shifted her gaze to a short, thin, ebony-skinned bellhop hurrying to Reggie's side of the car. "Your friend left a note for you."

The driver pushed his hand into his pocket and retrieved a fifty-cent piece. After taking the envelope, Reggie flipped the coin to the bellhop and said, "Thanks."

"O'Toole?" Bobbs asked.

"Couldn't use my own name," Reggie explained as he opened the envelope and read the note.

"Is it from Clay?" Meeker asked.

"Yes, and it looks like we won't be going to our rooms after all. We're supposed to meet him."

"Where?" the team leader asked.

"At Anthony Corelle's estate. It's out of town on something called the French Bayou. It seems my brother and his friend are Mr. Corelle's guests. Lassies, we might be about to find out a great deal more about the man New Orleans fears as much as the devil himself. And in the process, if Clay's description is right, the man with Alistar is the same man who held me prisoner."

CHAPTER 21

Friday, May 15, 1942
10:00 AM
New Orleans, Louisiana

An evening of food and music was followed by a restless night with very little sleep. Though his boss hadn't shown any reaction, Alistar was spooked by both the information they'd received from Nichols and spotting Clay Barnes. In his estimation the best thing to do was to get out of town and wait until things cooled down. Over a large southern-style breakfast, he attempted to get his boss to reconsider going to the Corelle estate. Even as the two climbed in what had once been the professor's Packard station wagon, Alistar begged Bauer to reconsider. Eight miles later, with New Orleans far behind and the sights and smells of the bayou all around, the large eight-cylinder car pulled to a stop in front of a dark, foreboding two-story home, and Alistar realized there would be no turning back.

"Looks like a place of black magic," he noted as he shut off the motor. "You're crazy," Bauer shot back. "Don't you realize only fools buy into superstition?"

"Then call me a fool."

"I have—more times that I can count." Bauer got out of the car and quickly moved up the brick walk toward the front door. He stopped only when he realized his companion was not by his side. Turning back he called softly, "I thought you wanted to sample some of the water from the fountain of youth."

"I do," Alistar replied, still standing beside the car, "but you don't think it's real." "Ah," Bauer said with a sly smile, "you want to believe it. You figure that water is the one way to get my grip off your life and soul. If it's real you can kill me. But you don't have the guts to find out."

He was right; Alistar did want to get rid of Bauer. He wanted it worse than anything in the whole world, but suddenly meeting with the man seemingly controlling that water didn't appeal to him.

"You coming?" Bauer asked.

What choice did he have? Corelle could kill him just as easily in front of the house as inside the place. Sticking his hands in his pocket, Alistar answered, "Yeah, sure."

Without hesitation Bauer knocked on the tall double doors of the century-old Creole-style, two-story stone mansion and waited for a response. A white-haired black servant, after asking their business, ushered the pair into a large library decorated in a style that went out of date a century before. Everything in the room, from the plush velvet-covered chairs and couches to the lamps, looked as though they came out of a French palace during the reign of Louis XIV.

"I will get Mr. Corelle," the old man announced as he left the two alone.

Still concerned about meeting the legendary man, Alistar was nevertheless caught by the lavish surroundings. From its oriental carpeting to the heavy dark furniture, the room reeked of money. "Corelle has unique taste," he noted as he studied a six-by-four- foot brass-framed oil portrait hanging over an even larger fireplace.

Bauer looked away from the books lining the shelves on the inside wall and observed, "I don't know if you've realized it, but there's nothing in this room from this century. Mr. Corelle evidently lives in the past."

"He might actually be from the past," a suddenly hopeful Alistar chimed in.

Seemingly unconcerned Bauer picked up a novel called *Say and Seal* and settled into an oversized, high-backed velvet-covered chair. As he opened the book, he off- handedly suggested, "You might as well relax. This is New Orleans, and nothing moves quickly down here."

Alistar glanced up to the mantel clock to check the time before settling into a straight-backed walnut chair beside a massive desk. Carved into both the chair and desk were scores of faces with one thing in common—they seemed to be screaming in terror. Apprehensively looking around he noted that same theme everywhere. Edgar Allen Poe, if he'd visited the estate, would have put the room into one of his stories. An hour later Bauer was fifty pages into his book and Alistar had counted more than 153 ghoulish faces in the woodwork. As an old clock chimed the hour, he noted, "I think they've forgotten us."

"No," Bauer assured him. "They know we're here. Someone will see us at some point. And here's something you need to remember: powerful men always keep people waiting. It's a test of will. They want to see how the passing of time affects you. The more comfortable you are, the more you use the given moments in some constructive fashion, such as reading, the more respect they'll have for you. And the longer you stay without complaint, the more certain they are that you're serious about your reasons for seeing them."

The explanation had no more than come out of Bauer's thin lips than the twelve- foot walnut door connected to the front foyer opened. On the other side was a slightly built man, likely in his forties. His hair was jet black, his skin tan, his eyes shimmering pieces of coal. Dressed in a pink cotton shirt and light blue linen pants, he studied the two guests for a moment before stepping forward.

"I am Jacques Corelle." His baritone voice was strong but not overpowering. "I understand you've come to this house to discuss business."

"My name is Sims," Bauer lied as he set the book to one side and stood. "I'm a banker. My associate is from the United Kingdom, and his name is Brewster. We had hoped to speak to

Anthony Corelle."

"No one speaks to my great grandfather without an appointment," Jacques explained. "If there's something he needs to know, I'll share it with him. And as I run the business affairs of this family, I'm a busy man. So make your point."

Alistar studied Bauer to see how their host's abrupt manner affected him. If he was perturbed, he didn't show it. In fact he wore a rare smile.

"Mr. Corelle, we are interested in a piece of property that your family owns outside of Mountain View, Arkansas. We would like to make you an offer on it."

The small man frowned. "The Corelles were given it by the King of France even before the United States made the Louisiana Purchase. Thomas Jefferson honored our claim to the property. It's not for sale, today or ever. You've wasted my time and yours."

Bauer nodded. "I understand sentimental value. I still own land in Germany that's been in my family since the fourteenth century, but I do have a price. For the right amount of money, I would sell. I'm sure I can offer you a princely sum that would be at the very least tempting. You see, money for me is no object."

"There is no price that could buy that land. Now if there's nothing else, may I show you out?"

Bauer waved his hand. "I understand on the property, but before we leave could you tell me about the portrait over the mantle? I rarely see that quality in modern oils." Their host smiled and walked toward the fireplace. As Bauer joined him

Alistar stepped to the window and gazed out onto the grounds. Beyond a stand of moss-covered trees, he noted a one-and-a-half ton truck, its bed covered, pulling up to a small stone building. After opening the door to the structure, a large broad-shouldered driver opened the tailgate, pulled off a series of wooden barrels, and one by one rolled them inside the building.

Looking back toward his boss and their host, Alistar announced, "While you discuss art, I hope you'll excuse me. I'm going to head back to the car for a smoke. I trust no one has any objections."

"Fine with me," Bauer assured him.

When their host offered no objection, Alistar hurried from the room and out the front door. After making sure no one was looking, he made his way around the side of the mansion and toward the stone building. The driver was just raising the tailgate when the visitor arrived.

"Hello," Alistar announced with a wave.

"Don't think I know you," came the tense response.

"We're visiting the Corelle family." He looked from the truck to the building before asking, "How was your drive from Arkansas?"

"How did you know?"

Alistar's eyes locked onto the man. "You go there every month for the water." He paused and grinned. "Have you ever taken a drink of the stuff? Is it really that good?"

"No one drinks it except the Corelles. Those are the rules. The only man I know of who tried it died within a week."

"The water's poison?"

"No. The man died from lead poisoning. He was shot twelve times." "Just for taking a drink?"

"Those are the rules. He knew his fate when he popped the lid off a jug."

"So you've never been tempted?" Alistar asked. "After all, isn't your cargo why the old man is still alive?"

The man froze in place, seemingly unsure how to answer the question. Sensing the driver might alert someone else, Alistar reached under his light jacket and pulled out a pistol complete with a silencer. "I promise you won't be shot a dozen times. Once or twice ought to do."

The driver never had a chance to yell out for help. With no warning Alistar squeezed the trigger twice, and the man fell lifeless to the ground. After returning his gun to its holster, the shooter dragged the driver over to the shed, reached into the dead man's pockets, retrieved a set of keys, and found the one fitting the lock to the shed. After the door was open, he dragged the victim inside and switched on a light. The room was filled with barrels as well as shelves of glass gallon jugs. Grabbing a bottle Alistar tore off the cork top and lifted it to his lips. As the liquid drained down his throat, he felt like the most powerful man on the planet. After laughing, he drained another eight ounces, then stepped outside and looked around. It appeared no one had spotted him.

Retracing his steps back into the shed, he looked down at the man he'd just shot. Kneeling he took the jug and splashed some in the victim's mouth. A second later the driver's eyes opened.

"Amazing," Alistar whispered. "It can even wake the dead."

"Please," the man cried out.

"I know you were dead. I hit you twice in the heart. It really does work. This is amazing!"

As the horrified man watched, Alistar got up, yanked out the gun, and pumped two more rounds into the driver. This time the bullets hit the forehead. Putting the weapon back in place, Alistar turned his attention to the job at hand. The clock was ticking, and he was going to have to move fast.

As if possessed he loaded a dozen barrels back onto the truck; for good measure he placed a half-dozen jugs in the passenger seat and onto the floorboard. Wiping the sweat from his brow, he took another sip from the already opened jug before hurrying back across the grounds to the front door. After opening it he quietly walked to the library, opened the door, and stepped into the room. Bauer and Jacques were still beside the fireplace, talking about the artist and his unique style, when they noticed his return.

"I guess you got tired of waiting on me," Bauer said.

"You could say that," Alistar replied. "In fact I don't think I'll be waiting ever again."

Without warning Alistar yanked out his gun and pulled the trigger; Jacques Corelle fell to the ground without a sound.

"Are you crazy?" Bauer screamed.

"Your hold over me is gone." Alistar's announcement was framed by a wry grin. "You see, I've tasted the water. In fact I have a large supply waiting for me outside. I don't need your fix now, and I don't need you."

Bauer shook his head. "You don't actually believe that stuff, do you? It's nothing more than a legend. I can see a fool like Hitler buying it, but not you. I've taught you better than that."

"You don't have any power over me now," Alistar growled, "but I have the power I need to rid myself of you. I can't tell you how much I've looked forward to this moment. Do you want it in the head or the heart?"

Bauer frowned. "So nice of you to give me a choice. I'll take it in the heart."

Alistar grinned as he pulled the trigger two more times. His eyes filled with a mad glee as a second later the tall man groaned and crumpled to the floor. After taking a final look at the chaos he'd created, he turned, hurried from the room and out the front door, and then walked quickly across the grounds to the truck. Sliding into the driver's seat, he turned the key in the ignition, pushed down the floor starter, and smiled as the vehicle came to life. Shoving the Ford into first, he made a slow turn onto the lawn, circled under a moss-covered tree, and headed down the long lane toward the main road. He'd never felt more alive or free!

CHAPTER 22

Friday, May 15, 1942
11:30 AM
New Orleans, Louisiana

Hidden behind a stand of cypress trees just across the road from the Corelle mansion, Meeker and her team watched Alistar Fister dash across the grounds and duck out of sight beside the mansion. A minute later a large truck pulled into the lane and circled around the yard toward the front gate. Looking back toward the front door, the woman waited to see who followed. No one did.

"I think he's going solo," Barnes announced.

Bobbs nodded. "Those pops we heard coming from the house could have been made by a gun rigged with a silencer."

"Reggie, you come with me," Meeker ordered. "We're taking the car and following your brother. I'm not going to let him escape this time. Clay, you and Becca take a look at what's inside. Be careful; you don't know who's alive or how many there are in the house. When we get Alistar, we'll come back and pick you up."

Meeker raced over to the tan sedan and slipped into the driver's seat. The Scottish member of her team was close behind.

"Hang on," she cried out. He didn't even have the passenger door shut when the woman hit the gas and pulled out from behind a tree and onto the dirt road.

"Okay, Reggie, I trust you have a gun. I want to take your brother alive, but if he won't let us, then we'll do what we have to."

"I understand. I'm tired of him embarrassing me anyway."

The dust stirred up by the truck was hovering in the air as Meeker pushed the sedan to sixty. As the large commercial rig Alistair was driving likely had a top end of fifty, she wasn't concerned about catching up. In fact she figured it would take less than two minutes to get the truck in her sights. But when suddenly there was no dust or no fresh tracks on the dirt road, she felt her confidence slip. Where had he gone?

Meeker slowed the Ford to twenty to gauge what had happened. This area of the bayou was flat and the road was straight. She could see for at least a mile, and there was nothing in front of her.

"Where is he?" she whispered.

Glancing to her left she saw nothing but swamp. To her right was a flat, almost park-like area containing a stand of cypress, but neither offered a place for a truck to hide. She was about to slow to a stop and turn around when she caught something moving out of the corner of her eye.

"He's behind us!" Reggie yelled.

As the truck filled her mirror, she noted, "Must have pulled off and waited for us to go by. Hang on; he's going to try to ram us."

Meeker hit the gas, but it was a spilt-second too late. The ton-and-a-half truck's huge bumper hit the sedan hard, pushing it toward the swamp. Unable to control the steering, Meeker watched helplessly as a large cypress filled her windshield. The only thing that kept it from coming through the glass was the Ford's V-8 nose. As they struck the ancient tree, the sedan's sheet metal crumpled like tin foil, and Reggie was tossed headfirst into the dash. Meeker caught the steering wheel with her chest and stomach.

Regaining her senses, she looked over her shoulder just as a grinning Alistar, gun in hand, opened the truck's door and climbed out.

"Reggie, we have to get out of here," she screamed. When no one answered she glanced to her right. Her companion was either knocked out or dead. There was no time to figure out which.

Reaching into her pocket she felt for her Colt. It wasn't there. It must have fallen out when they hit the tree. She looked around the floorboard and spotted the gun. If she couldn't stand and fight, she'd have to run. Yanking the handle up, she pushed the door open with her shoulder and stumbled out onto the soft, marshy ground. As her shoe stuck in the soil, she looked back toward Alistar. He was standing behind her, smiling, his revolver in his right hand and a gallon jug in the other.

CHAPTER 23

Friday, May 15, 1942
12:10 PM
New Orleans, Louisiana

Clay Barnes and Becca Bobbs hadn't bothered knocking as they charged through Anthony Corelle's front door. An elderly black servant, his expression pained and his mouth ajar, stood to one side and pointed toward an open door. Needing no explanation the pair, guns drawn, quickly made their way into what appeared to be a library. By the fireplace was a body oozing blood from the head. After assessing the situation, Bobbs looked back to the servant and demanded, "Who's that?"

"Mr. Jacques Corelle," the man answered.

Barnes chimed in next. "There was a tall, thin man who came into the house. I didn't see him leave, so where is he?"

"He was here when I left this room," the old man explained, "but I haven't seen him since."

"Becca," Barnes announced as he scanned his surroundings, "the only other way out is through the far door."

"I'll check it out," she assured her partner. "Be careful. I'll cover you."

Bobbs hustled across the room and slipped the door open a few inches. "It leads to a back hall with stairs at the end."

"They go to the second floor bedrooms," the servant said.

Bobbs looked at her partner. "What's that on the floor beside you?"

Barnes reached down and picked up a square, gold-colored item and studied it briefly. "It's a cigarette case. And it has two dents, indicating it might have stopped a couple of slugs."

"Maybe that's the reason there's not more blood," Bobbs suggested. "Perhaps Corelle and this guy were caught up in a gun battle, and Corelle lost. If you're right then that cigarette case might have saved that man's life."

"Then were is he now?" Barnes asked. He glanced back to the servant. "Is there any chance the other visitor ran out of this room?"

The old man shook his head, still wide-eyed and visibly shaken.

Bobbs looked back to the door and the hall leading to the stairs. "Then there's only one way for him to go."

"You can't go up there," the servant stated, conviction in his tone. "No one is allowed up there."

"Why not?" Bobbs asked.

"That's the rule. I've worked here for forty years, and no one besides the Corelle family has ever walked those stairs. And no one sees Mr. Anthony except once a year when he comes down for Mardi Gras. Members of his family even take his meals to him."

Barnes looked over at Bobbs. "Well, it might be time for someone other than the family to make a visit."

"Why did Alistar bolt?" Barnes asked.

"Did you see a gun on Corelle?" she asked.

Barnes knelt beside the dead man's body and searched his clothing. He then rolled Corelle over to examine the carpet beneath him. Looking back at his partner, he shrugged. "No gun."

"That frames things differently," she replied. "This was a murder, not a gun battle, and I'm guessing Alistar pulled the trigger. But why?"

"Find the tall guy," Barnes suggested, "and we might answer that question."

Gun ready, the woman led the way through the door and mounted the stairs. One by one she climbed them, with her partner mirroring each of her moves. At the top was a long hallway—four doors on one side and four on the other. Bobbs signaled for Barnes to check the doors on the left of the six-foot wide corridor; she'd take the ones on the right. She held her place, weapon ready, as he twisted the first knob and pushed the door open. He waited, glanced in, and then took a step forward.

"Empty," he mouthed a few moments later.

Bobbs nodded and moved to the door opposite the first room.

Shifting her gun to her left hand, she twisted the knob and the door creaked open. The furnishings were old, the room musty and void of life. Leaving the entry open, the woman led the way to the next door and repeated her actions. The result was the same. Barnes' experience across the hall was identical too. There were four doors to go.

"What do you make of it?" she whispered.

"No one has lived in those rooms for years," he whispered back.

It was more than not living in the rooms; it was the fact the decorating style was literally from a different century. So the rooms hadn't been updated for decades. No new photographs, no magazines, nothing to tie them to the 1900s, much less 1942.

"This place is like a museum," she whispered. Pointing to the third room on the left, she stood to the side as Barnes pushed it open.

"No one home," he said a few seconds later, "but someone does live here. The bed's unmade, and there are clothes tossed on a chair."

As Bobbs stood in the entry, looking back toward the hall to assure that no one could surprise them, her partner continued his search.

"Becca," Barnes said in hushed tones, "based on the mail, this is Jacques' room. So we've found where the dead man hung his hat. I suggest you take a look across the hall. I'll come out and cover you."

Bobbs stepped forward and approached the next door. After

taking a deep breath, she pushed it open. The first thing she noted was a radio with a phone beside it, a stack of newspapers on a table, and a new issue of *Time Magazine* on the corner of the four-poster bed. Moving through the entry, she walked to a closet and slowly pulled that door open, finding nothing but clothing and shoes. Quietly moving to a round table standing between two wooden straight-backed chairs, she glanced down at an envelope before rejoining her partner.

"It appears," she whispered, "that a Marcus Corelle calls that room home, but based on the newspaper's dates, he hasn't been here in a few days."

Barnes' eyes moved to the final room on the left. "Guess it's my turn."

With Bobbs watching his every move, the man eased to the door and slowly twisted the brass knob. As it opened a black cat raced out and ran between his legs. Without looking back the creature streaked down the hall and to the stairs. After regaining the composure the feline had stolen from him, Barnes looked back into the room.

"No one's here either," he whispered. "Based on the clothing and perfume bottles, I'm guessing a woman lives in this one."

"We can look at it in greater detail later. For the moment let's find out if this final door leads us to Mr. Anthony Corelle."

Shifting her gun back to her right hand, Bobbs eased over to the entry, paused, looked back at her partner and, changing her tactics, knocked. When no one answered she repeated her actions. There was still no reply. With Barnes on her right, she twisted the knob and pushed the door open. The windows must have been covered to assure not even a speck of light made it in from outside. Feeling with her left hand, she found an old push-style light switch.

"You ready?" she asked her partner. "Go for it."

Only one overhead light came on; thus the scene displayed before them was filled with menacing shadows. Yet even in the dim light one thing was certain: this time they were not alone. A figure dressed in a dark suit, knee-high boots, and a large, black floppy hat sat in a chair in the far corner.

"Mr. Corelle?" Bobbs called out. There was no answer.

"I'm not here to hurt you," she assured him, "but we do need to talk." Corelle, his face hidden by the shadows, did not reply.

Bobbs glanced back to Barnes. After he nodded she moved slowly toward the mysterious figure, expecting the man to at least lift his hand to signal for her to stop. Yet for reasons she couldn't fathom, he remained stone still.

"Mr. Corelle," she said again, stopping just three feet in front of his chair, "answer me." The large hat still kept his face from her view, but she could now see the man wore gloves, and the fingers of his right hand were curled around an antique pistol. Keeping her eye on the weapon, Bobbs warned, "Leave the gun where it is."

Once again the man did not respond.

Just to Corelle's right, in the middle of an old table, sat a lamp. While keeping one eye on the man's gun, she reached out and yanked a chain barely visible under a green fabric shade.

A split-second later a yellow glow illuminated Mr. Anthony Corelle. His skin was leathery and dark, his eyes and cheeks sunken, and his lips drawn back in a smile revealing yellowed teeth. Yet he still didn't move.

"Is he dead?" Barnes asked from his position by the door.

Bobbs nodded. "Has been for many years. I'd bet he drew his last breath decades ago."

"It was all a charade," Barnes said, coming up to stand beside her. "It was just the family's way of holding onto power through the appearance of magic."

Bobbs continued to stare at Corelle. "And it worked." Turning toward Barnes she asked, "But what happened to the tall man you saw enter the home with Alistar?"

"He must have slipped away."

"Or he's still hiding in one of the other rooms. Let's do a more thorough search." "What about Helen and Reggie?"

"I'm sure they can take care of themselves," the blonde replied.

CHAPTER 24

Friday, May 15, 1942
12:20 PM
New Orleans, Louisiana

Helen Meeker was well aware she couldn't outrun the bullets in Alistar Fister's gun, and with no weapon of her own, she was going to have to come up with another plan of escape. But what? A mouse caught in a snap-trap had more of a chance of releasing that powerful spring than she did of worming out of this mess. Attempting to stay calm, she looked past the man to the scene around her. Just to her right was the swamp, to her left a small wooded area, and behind her a dusty road leading two miles to the Corelle mansion. With Alistar's gun aimed squarely at her heart, those two miles might as well have been a million.

With no obvious escape routes open, her gaze turned back to Alistar just as he took a long swig from a glass jug. As the clear liquid dripped from the corner of his mouth and dropped down onto his jacket, he smiled.

"You must be really enjoying that drink."

Setting the clear container on the ground, he wiped his mouth with his sleeve and nodded. Sporting a crazy grin, his eyes wild, almost as if they were on fire, he chuckled. "Nothing has ever tasted any better."

She was puzzled. Why was he acting so strange? This was not the cool, aloof Alistar who'd once charmed even her. This man seemed more like a rebellious teenage

boy. Was he drunk? Was it the booze talking? Or maybe the blood doping had finally taken its toll on his brain.

"Helen," Alistar laughed, "you were the woman who turned me down, the love that got away, and the chick that flew the coup all rolled into one. It wasn't hard pretending I was in love. You're beautiful. How many times have I thought about you since that first night we met at the embassy? How many times have I wondered what it would have been like if you hadn't resisted my charms in your apartment? I almost had you that night; you have to admit that."

Perhaps if she pushed him hard enough, reminding him of the prize he lost, he might want to hold her and kiss her again. And if he tried he might be close enough for her to have the chance to wrestle his gun away from him and turn the tables.

"You don't have to look to the past anymore; I'm here. Now what are you going to do about it? You weren't man enough to take me that night. Are you now?"

He grinned. "Things have changed since then, Helen. After

all, it was my blood that saved you." She cocked her right eyebrow as he continued. "You must hate knowing my blood gave you a second chance at life."

"I'm not thrilled with it," she admitted, "and I'm guessing it won't save me now.

But at least admit the truth. You still want me."

"Maybe, but the fact you have my blood running through your veins makes you seem like the sister I never had. And who really has any desire to kiss a sister?"

An unexpected splash caused Meeker and Alistar to look into the swamp. A ten- foot gator swam to within fifty feet of the bank, stopped with his eyes just above the murky water, and stared at them.

"You'll be a tasty treat for him," Alistar said. "I might be a little tough," Meeker quipped.

"You're a piece of work!" Alistar laughed. "Most women would be begging for their lives, but not you. You're just egging me on."

"I'll bet you like pulling the wings off flies." She smirked. "By the way, what happened to your buddy back at the mansion? I'm assuming he was the man who ordered both you and Grace Lupino around."

"Grace didn't resist my charms. I actually believed she fancied me. But it's hard to say with any certainty as she used people just like I did. You know, two people who lack any sense of conscience really don't make a very good couple. You see, not only did we use each other, but we were also constantly trying to find out how much it would be worth to sell the other one out."

"I've met you both," Meeker chimed in, "and I'd take ten Lupinos over one Alistar Fister. Now what happened to the puppet master?"

"I killed him. I don't need him anymore. I don't need his injections. I have the water now, and I know where I can get more."

What was he talking about? She glanced from the glass jug back to the man. Had he completely lost his mind?

"Ah, Helen, my beautiful lassie, I now have Anthony Corelle's secret. Life is simply wonderful, and it will go on and on and on." He laughed again. "You know what living forever makes me?"

"What?" she asked, still confused by the man's seeming lack of focus. "A god. And gods don't have seizures. Those are behind me now."

The gator, which had been stationary in the middle of the pool, now moved slowly and almost silently closer to the shore. As his tail swished in the water, he came within twenty feet of where Meeker was standing.

"About those seizures," she said. "Grace told me about them."

"Yeah, they're no fun. It was—" He interrupted his own thought. "Isn't *was* a nice word? Anyway, it *was* just a side-effect. Now those days are over."

"So the formula's been perfected?"

"No, but I have been. I have in my possession what millions

have looked for. I have what Ponce De Leon wanted. I have youth and eternal life forever in my grasp." He smiled. "Grace knows the price of the injections. She saw what they did to me. And as you have my blood flowing through your body, it will affect you too. Let me correct myself. It would affect you *if* I let you live long enough for it to wreak havoc on your system. And it would give me so much pleasure to watch the great Helen Meeker lose control. I'd pay a lot of money for a show like that."

"If you kill me now," she taunted, "you'll always wonder what it was like to have me . . . to really have me."

"I don't want a good girl." He laughed yet again. "They're no fun."

Meeker nodded, her dark blue eyes glancing toward the still floating gator and back to the man whose toothy grin made him appear just as dangerous. As he watched, her right hand began to shake. "What's happening?" Meeker screamed, causing both Alistar and the alligator to look her direction. Clutching her left hand to her throat, she began to tremble. "What's going on?" she whispered. Falling to her knees in the grass, she reached for the car to keep from collapsing flat on the ground. That kept her steady for a moment, but then the trembles morphed into shaking so powerful her head banged into the Ford's door.

"My blood!" Alistar chortled. "It's got you. You're helpless! I get to watch it after all."

Meeker tried to push up off the ground but only managed to lift her knees a few inches before crumpling into a writhing heap. "What's going on?" she moaned. "Alistar, please help me.

Please!"

The man came to within five feet of the woman before glancing back to the gator. "You have him interested," Alistar said. "He senses you're weak and wounded. As soon as I walk away, he'll come get you and drag you back into the water. Maybe he'll pull you under and drown you before he starts to tear you apart. Still, I shouldn't take a chance on unproven help. He might just swim off rather than do the job I want him to do. And I couldn't take a chance on your living."

Meeker pushed her head off the ground and focused on the man. Her lips struggled to find words, but she couldn't manage anything more than a weak moan. He grinned and aimed his gun at her head.

"I'll get to kill my two greatest enemies in the same hour," he muttered. "How sweet is that?"

It was now or never. Meeker gathered her remaining strength and lunged forward in an attempt to grab the man's leg. It was a long shot that she could bring him to the ground before he pulled the trigger, but what other choice did she have? She was just about to make her move when the gator beat her to it. With no warning he shot out of the swamp and up on the bank. Turning, Alistar straightened his arm and fired. The bullet hit the beast in the back causing him to shrink back into the water.

Straightening his arm, he turned and aimed at Meeker. Still shocked by the gator's move, she couldn't respond quickly enough. Before she tried to move forward, he squeezed the trigger, but this time it only clicked. A second attempt brought the same results. After a long series of curses, he said, "Out of bullets." Shrugging he looked to the wounded alligator floating just a few feet off shore. "I guess I'll just let the big guy get the pleasure of draining the life from you. I think I can trust him to enjoy his work."

Laughing, Alistar turned on his heels and with long, deliberate steps, walked back to the truck, leaned down, picked up the jug, took another sip of water, and looked out at the swamp. "She's all yours, boy. I've already paid for your meal." Alistar looked back to the fallen woman. "Your friends will no doubt be here very soon, and I can't afford to get caught in a gunfight with them. It seems my extra ammunition is still back in my hotel room. Maybe, if they're real lucky, they'll find an arm or a leg and figure out what happened to you."

Sliding into the truck Alistar slammed the door, fired up the motor, slipped the vehicle into gear, and leaned his head out the window. "Bon appetite!" Pushing gently on the gas, he steered the old truck down the dusty road. Meeker watched the vehicle disappear before rolling her head back toward the swamp. The bleeding gator was moving steadily her way, and he appeared hungry.